Tyrant's Gallow

Moonsong, Book II

By
David V. Stewart

©2014-2020 David V Stewart. All rights reserved. All persons depicted herein are fictitious. Any resemblance to any person, living or dead, is purely coincidental.
Cover design and © by David V. Stewart.
Cover assets by Algol, skiserge1, Veronika, olenadesign, Zacarias da Mata, F.C.G., faestock, Shutter2U, and Fotokvadrat
Map by David V. Stewart ©2020
Body Font: Arno Pro
Headline Font: Trajan Pro 3
Dropcap font: Goudy Initialen

Contents

Map of The North Pelagian vii

Interlude II: Divinity 1

I: Nantien 8

II: The Gallow 18

III: No Strangers 29

IV: Lords of Legend 43

V: The Golden Palace 54

VI: Entries and Episodes 69

VII: Gold Courthouse 83

VIII: Games of Chance 95

IX: The Goods 112

X: Into the Dark 129

XI: Down and Out 141

XII: The Business 154

XIII: Shoals 168

XIV: Greyskins 184

About the Author 204

For Houkje

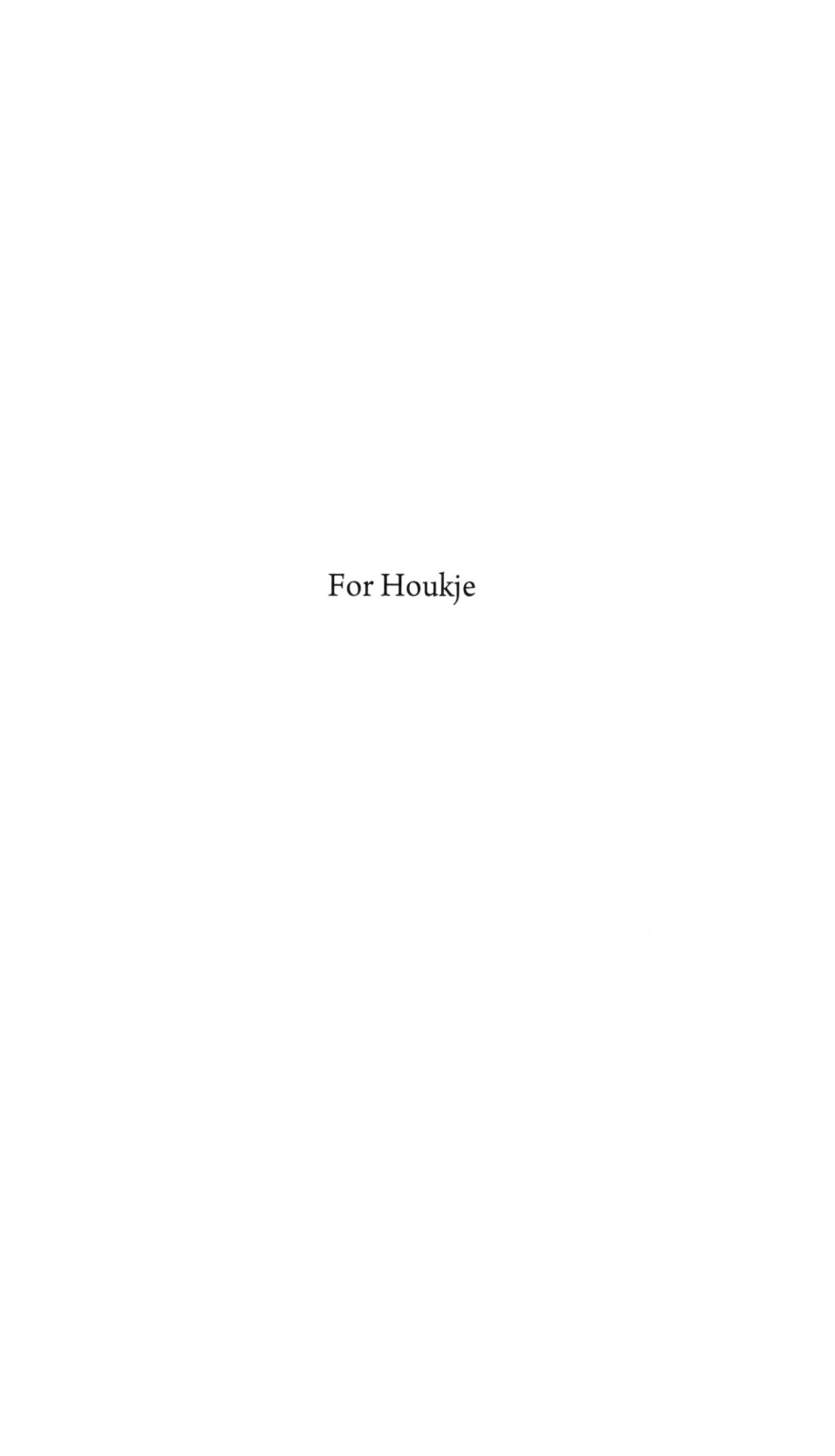

The North
Pelagian
In the Sixth Dominion

Tyrant's Gallow

Interlude II: Divinity

Claire stood at the edge of the castle chapel, staring through a clear space in one of the windows. The image of the shore beyond was blurry through the ancient glass. The sun cast on her face and the floor about her a multitude of colors. She sighed.

"You're looking rather morose."

Claire startled and then quickly dropped to a knee and bowed before the Grand Cleric, who stood before her already arrayed in his robes of office bearing two red stripes, but not yet wearing his heavy iron crown. He was a man that, had he been a commoner, would have been considered old; his hair and beard were grey and his face was lined with wrinkles. As clergy, his sixty years was well short of even retirement age.

"Apologies, master Gibson," Claire said, spreading her robes about her, covering her feet in a gesture of modesty few in Veraland would recognize. Gibson touched her hair lightly, and she looked up to see his smiling face.

"It is good to see you, Claire," he said. "I have spent too long enduring the company of seamen and temple guardians. Please rise, my friend." He held out a hand, and she took it as she stood up again. He squeezed it softly before he released it. "Yes, it is good to have the company of a friend once again."

Claire nodded. "Likewise, master. I have missed the company of the cloth."

"Come now, Claire, I am speaking of friendship, not of camaraderie, though I hope we will ever strive for the same purposes."

"Of course, my apologies."

"No more apologies and no more titles, Claire." He turned and began walking casually through the double doors into the circular castle chapel, as large as any church on the Isle, and twice as richly decorated. A large clock was set into the center altar, displaying three o'clock. "Here, in the church, we are friends, if not equals."

Claire smiled at him.

"I had a chance to drop in on your daughter some months ago. She is learning well, despite her age, as I knew she would."

"Good. Is she happy?"

"Yes, I think so. She has a small cadre of friends. They are more concerned with the boys from the art school than their own education, but they are good friends. The boys... well, they are good, too. I may arrange a courtship for Maribel with one that has a particular eye for architecture that I expect to work for the church one day."

"You know my heart too well, Gibson," Claire said. She glanced at the clock. "The count and heir apparent should be here at four if you wish to receive him."

"I do." For clergy as high as a Grand Cleric, second only to the Hand of the Divine, kings did not *command* audience. Kings were *admitted* to the cleric's presence at his discretion.

"He will be accompanied by his minister of war."

"I had anticipated this."

"Then you know that Charlotte has gone missing."

Gibson paused and turned to Claire, frowning and puzzled. "No, I did not know this." He shook his head. "War... yes, I knew of that. I was to coronate him, I thought. That would demand the lady as well."

"You arrived quickly. News travels fast. I assumed you knew everything."

"For me, it travels fast. I had not anticipated Grasslund's

death, just so you know."

"I wouldn't accuse you."

Gibson nodded and looked to the ornate altar that sat at the center of the lofty room. Gilded representations of the twelve gods faced in a circle. Verbus, the god of death and words, faced the entranceway. Claire felt a shiver as she looked at the god's carved chin. His eyes were obscured by a hood.

Gibson sighed. "What will be my errand here, now? I cannot legally crown a king and not his queen. There are many words in the divine texts that can be bent, or even ignored, but not that one. Not when the nobility is already testing their relationship with the church. I must be firm."

"Perhaps we can say Charlotte was killed in her escape."

"What?" Gibson's frown deepened as he looked down on Claire.

Claire hesitated and took a deep breath. "We conclude that she was killed, then Sarthius will be free to remarry and receive the crown. The queen in the Green Isle is, at best, a figurehead."

"Your suggestion is not what shocked me. Indeed, it is a practical solution, if a bit prone to some distasteful speculation by the lesser gentry." His frown deepened. "No, you said she escaped. *Escaped.* What do you mean by this?"

Claire felt her pulse quicken as she realized her slip. "We are friends." She did not pose it as a question, but the silence turned it into one.

"You can trust me." Gibson's blue eyes burned at Claire, but their intensity came not from anger, but something else further inside. Claire thought it looked like fear or anxiety – deep an sincere.

"Charlotte of the Plain did not abide her station," Claire said. "Thrice she sent pleas to King Vegard of Hviterland, her uncle, requesting suit for annulment or divorce. I know this because Sarthius Catannel intercepted and held all these letters. Only the first was sent openly, in naïve belief Charlotte's seal would be respected."

"It should have been."

"But you know the nobility as well as I," Claire said. She collapsed into a chair beside a pew and let her brown hair fall around her face. Gibson let himself down onto a nearby bench. "I do not blame her, Gibson. I cannot. What Sarthius did... what he *does* to... others. It is very vicious. *Very* vicious."

"Will you not say more?"

"I cannot. I dare not, even if I knew everything. What I do know would turn your stomach and turn your hair white even without your years. Spend a night out of your robes in a common room in the city below. The rumors will not be far from the truth." A hand rested on her leg lightly, and she looked up to see Gibson, his eyes trembling.

"What has he done to you, Claire?"

"To me?" Claire shook her head and let out a sigh. "Not what you are thinking. He has despoiled me of my integrity, of my security, of most my worth to you and to our church, but he has not despoiled me of *that*, Gibson. I am in no danger there."

"I will quietly re-assign you."

"No!" Claire said. Her voice boomed in the hall. As the echo died, another set of doors opened, and the sounds of Gibson's attendees filled the silence. Claire spoke a soft growl, "No, that will do no good. Not for me, and not for my daughter. And not for whoever you send in to replace me in this chapel. Here I can do good. I can guide, I can push, even if it is a bit impotent. I can observe and report. And I can betray if needed. It is best to keep me here, Gibson."

Gibson nodded. "The snares of the nobility can be cruel. We view Sarthius as a useful tool, if a cruel one. I apologize for his necessity."

Claire nodded back. "So many tangles." She looked up to the altar, her eyes almost glazed. "You had a nice boy in mind for Maribel?"

"There are many boys that are nice and years yet to introduce them."

Claire smiled. The attendants began to file in, their colorful uniforms bright in the placid chapel. "Good. We are nearing the time, your grace. You will need your crown to receive the king in his dedication to you."

*

Sarthius Cattanel scratched his freshly shaven chin and examined himself in the mirror. He wore the livery of a coronation: a long plush cape enveloped his shoulders and trailed behind him on the carpet. His hose and shined shoes stood a stark black beside the white and gold of his trousers and jacket. He flicked his long fingers, and gold rings clacked together.

"You look excellent, sire," Blotella said. She stood nearby, her hands on her hips. A smile cracked her wrinkled face. "You have a good frame for a king."

"Image can have such power if you frame it right. That's the trick, though. Framing the image. Controlling who sees it, to produce the effect you desire."

Blotella looked puzzled, then bent down to adjust part of the taper of the cape. "We'll want to tack this in a bit before the actual coronation."

"I think I rather like it as it is," Sarthius said. "In fact, I intend to wear it now."

Behind him, Lord Marcus Grantell grumbled. Sarthius turned to look at his minister of war with curious, raised eyebrows.

"My apologies," Marcus said. He leaned his girth back, straining the buttons on the front of his military jacket. His black beard, flecked with grey, stood out from his chin stiff and waxed.

"I expect you to make your feelings understood, not felt," Sarthius said.

"Noted," Marcus said.

Sarthius felt a pang of frustration. Marcus was, until the coronation proper, on equal footing as a titled landowner, and he intended for Sarthius to know it. Though his estate contained only a few small villages and he was as distant from the throne as most peasants, he was still high nobility according to law.

"Well, what is your consternation about?"

"Wearing that get-up to be received by the High Cleric," Marcus said. "It sends a message that we do not need right now."

"That I am the proper king? But I am."

"*That* you are, but you are not being crowned today."

"But I should be. That is the message."

"The cleric will view you as overly ambitious. Unwilling to submit to the supremacy of the church."

"Of course he will."

Marcus pursed his lips.

Sarthius chuckled. "It is all part of the game, Marcus. We must seem dangerous for the church to view us as a powerful tool, and we must seem corruptible for them to want to control us."

Marcus nodded, chewing the inside of his lip.

"But of course, Marcus, it is *us* who will use *them*. But they mustn't think that."

"You're playing at a game the church has mastered for the better part of forty centuries."

"And the nobility has played that game with them." Sarthius turned and swept his cape, unmindful of the seamstress at his feet. "Come, let us set our benefactors on edge." Marcus hesitated to stand, and Sarthius widened his sardonic smile. "You must trust me, Marcus. Veraland shall be yours in time."

*

The ceremony – the coronation that was not – took place with nothing but proper pomp. Sarthius Catannel dressed as a king, though he was not one, and walked proudly beside his minister of war who was not a minister, since only the king could make such appointments. Marcus Grantel, standing erect in his formal jacket, was the kind of choice for a war office that only the most ambitious king would make. The Crow of the Highlands was known for his ruthlessness as much as his cunning. Rumors circulated constantly of his butchery. He had left bloodied bodies where they fell and dined of the field of battle after slaughtering the remnants of the southern Highland Clans, watching his favorite carrion birds have their much-loved supper of heretic eyes and tongues. Many enemies had he made in the southern reaches of the Isle, and not just among the farm folk that descended from the Dream worshippers of old. High Lord Bautchel had famously placed a price upon Marcus's head for three years, withdrawing it only at the behest of the now-dead King Graslund.

Only a man intending to *use* a weapon like the Crow would place Marcus Grantel in such a high position of power.

Claire turned these things over in her mind as she stood to the side of the Grand Cleric and watched the bowing and careful recitation of ancient, now nearly empty, words. Nobody acknowledged Sarthius's gesture of royalty, not even Sarthius himself. The king-that-would-be wore his smile as the ceremony passed into conventional conversation. Claire felt sick looking at that smile, and all that she imagined that it hid.

I: Nantien

he echoing thud of heavy footsteps woke Charlotte from her fitful sleep. Dreams of a great void surrounding the ship, bearing it through an ocean of dread toward a field of strange stars, faded into the reality of the sea and its constant sway. She felt the unwelcome return of the slight nausea that had plagued her since her escape from Masala.

Amid the chaotic percussion shaking the ceiling, she could hear voices, but the words were too muffled to be understood. She rose slowly from the straw mattress, rubbing her eyes and trying focus in the darkness of the small cabin. She still wore her white gown; a few light spots showed on the formerly pristine silk. She drew a blanket around herself, stood up, and cracked the door. Rone stood on the stairs outside, his arms crossed and cradling a musket. A flickering oil lamp hung on a nearby hook.

"What is it?" she said. Rone glanced at her before looking back out the door above him.

"Ship ahead. We're likely right on it to be seeing it at night and in the rain."

"Why is everyone scrambling?"

"We don't know if they are friendly or not. Is your rifle loaded?"

"Yes, I think so. You think there will be fighting?"

"As likely as not." He glanced at her again. "You should be dressed."

Charlotte turned back to the room and began hurriedly

assembling her clothes by the lamplight leaking through the cracks in the door. She paused as she pulled off her gown; she imagined Rone's eyes upon her naked back and felt a strange unease. A sort of silence had settled between them since Masala, and Rone never brought up the kiss they had shared – that she had *stolen*. She stepped back toward the door and shut the last inch of it, plunging her into total darkness. By touch, she pulled on her trousers and the faded, rough shirt she had grown to hate over the past weeks.

Charlotte checked the prime on her rifle's lock with a finger, nodded to herself, and went back to the door. When she opened it, Rone was gone, so she hurried up the steps to the main deck. Outside, the small crew stood crowded toward the gunwale. A scrawny young sailor continued to howl from the crow's nest above them.

"All I can see is fire!"

"Can you see the island or not? Is it only ships?" Pierce was standing on the main deck, with hands on his hips, shirtless despite the cold mist coating every surface. The sky on the other side of the crowd glowed orange. She picked out Rone's silhouette, his wide-brimmed hat giving him away in the gloom.

"I think I see buildings. I'm not sure!" the sailor in the crow's nest called back.

A door slammed behind Charlotte and she turned to see Johnny walking out of his cabin with a large spyglass in one hand and an unbelted cutlass in the other.

"Out of the way!" he growled. The crowd of men parted to let him walk up to the forecastle.

"Cap'n on deck!" Pierce called, but none of the men seemed to care.

Johnny's spyglass had a massive front objective on it and telescoped out to a length too great to hold. He threw down his cutlass and rested the spyglass on a rail. Johny's immense hight forced him to lean over almost double to look into it. While Johnny scanned the horizon, Rone followed Pierce up the stairs and stood behind the captain; there was a strange sight in the distance.

"Shit. Looks like a regular battle is taking place." Big Johnny pulled away from the eyepiece and raised an eyebrow. He waved at Rone. "Come here."

Rone stepped forward and bent over to look into the spyglass, which Johnny continued to hold against the rail. Rone pulled away for a moment, squinting and blinking, before looking through it again.

Charlotte pushed her way gently through the crew, shielding her eyes from the mist. The ship rocked hard as she pulled herself up to the gunwale, and she would have fallen had Pierce not seen her slipping and grabbed her arm at the last moment. It seemed a bright fire blazed in the distance, but she couldn't tell what was burning. Charlotte could, however, hear the droning report of canons over water.

"The whole port is on fire, it looks like," Rone said, leaning back to look at Johnny. "Not so much a naval battle as a sacking, I'd say."

"I didn't ask you to look because I'm blind. Do you recognize the ships?" Johnny said. He let go of the spyglass and turned away, looking to the crow's nest with his arms out for some kind of input. The man up top didn't answer.

Rone looked back into the glass.

"Most of the ships aren't flying colors," he said. "Those that are have a yellow stripe on some kind of dark-colored field. It's hard to see."

"That's the flag of Nantien's fleet," Johnny said.

"They've been routed," Rone said. "I see a few trying to abandon the port. Most are in flames."

"What about the other ships?" Johnny asked.

Rone was silent a moment. "Those ships are galleys, and an older style, too. Draesen Imperial warships or I'm a fool."

"What?"

"Never seen one?"

Johnny grumbled. "It's been about twenty years. You sure?"

"It's the right type. I can see the shadows of oars."

Rone stood up and handed the spyglass back to Johnny. Johnny hunched down again and looked back out to the sea of fire.

Rone caught sight of Charlotte and stepped toward her. With a smile, he took his hat off and placed it on her head.

"It seems trouble comes ahead of you, as well as behind," he said, pushing up the brim of the hat to reveal Charlotte's eyes. "That's Nantien. Or was"

Charlotte looked out over the black waters, ripples of black nothing like those in her dreams, though they filled her with the same feeling. The clouds above the island reflected the battle like a dim red sunrise.

"I'll be damned," Johnny said. "I think you've got to be right. What are they doing all the way out here? Can't be a slave raid."

"That doesn't make any sense," Pierce said. "Draesen? They would have to have sailed through the entire Barrier Sea. That's a thousand leagues of hotly contested water, with Datalian Navy and corporate frigates swarming all the ports."

"Unless they came another way," Rone said with a shrug. Johnny turned around and looked at him, hotness in his gaze.

"A campaign?" the captain said. He looked away for a protracted few moments. "It could be, at that. But in the north?"

"I don't see how it could be anything else," Rone said.

"The tundra will be melting," Charlotte said, watching the fires. "They could be sailing to the Northmarch. May I look?" A memory from her distant childhood hovered on the edge of her mind, blurry and yet stark. It was an image of a strange-looking man with inhuman skin and eyes.

Rone turned back and frowned at her, but did not inquire more. He nodded to the spyglass.

Charlotte bent down and put the glass to her eye. After a few moments of searching, she caught the sight of the battle

What she saw was spectacular. A fleet of ships moved in and out of focus, drifting past each other. Cannons lit up randomly along the heavy sides of warships. Sails were on fire and withering. Entire ships were ablaze, raging as they sank. Behind the battle, she could see a port town leaning up against a large black hill, lit by dozens of fires. Flames shot up suddenly from one of the buildings on the water. She could see small shadows – people, though they looked more like ants, or fleas – running through the backdrop of yellow and red. The burning building, a fortress of some sort, suddenly grew bright. A wall collapsed, and a great black and red cloud mushroomed into the sky.

"Do you recognize the ships, too?" Rone said.

Charlotte stood back up and rubbed her eye. "I don't know anything about ships. I was hoping to see one of… them."

"A Draesen?" Rone said.

"Yes."

"We'd have to get a lot closer to see people," Rone said.

"I'm not getting any closer to see them, and I'm not sticking around to find out why they're here," Johnny said. "Hard to port!"

"You mean starboard?" Rone said. "Golice is east."

"Hard to port, I say!" He looked at Rone with a slight smile as he picked up and collapsed the massive spyglass. "You can trust me to sail. We'll be far too hard-pressed to make it to Golice undermanned and with most of our supplies sitting on the dock in Masala."

"Bergan is east, too."

"Bergan? Boy, it's been plagued for a quarter year. Haven't you heard?" Johnny looked Rone in the eye and spat off the bow. He withdrew a compass from his waistcoat and flicked it. "Turn us to two-hundred sixty degrees!" He looked over at the wheel to see that it was unmanned and roped tight. He grumbled and sighed. "I have to do bloody everything around here, eh?"

"Where are we going?" Charlotte called out as Johnny stomped down the stairs.

"Tyrant's Gallow," Johnny said. He didn't look back, but Charlotte was sure he was smiling.

*

The usual dinner Rone and Charlotte had with the captain was quiet, the only sounds for a long time being the scraping of forks on the captain's rough personal plates. The whole crew had been silent for most of the day as they left Nantien, and whatever conflict had consumed it, behind. Improving weather had not lifted the mood that hung on the ship like a layer of fog.

"Do you really want to take the ship to the lion's den?" Charlotte said once the food was almost finished.

"If it's the lion's den, then I'm a lion," Johnny said, abandoning his fork and the soft vegetables there and leaning his chair back. He drew long on his pipe, the glow from which lit his eyes in a dark red hue. He blew out a large smoke ring above him, which disappeared as it hit the cold ceiling of the cabin.

"There's no king there," Charlotte said. "No law. Rampant sorcery, heresy, and…" Johnny started to laugh. Charlotte grumbled and turned away, feeling suddenly foolish and hot in the face.

"Cannibals? Human sacrifice? Old tales for children, dear,"

Johnny said.

"The crew won't tell you they don't like it, but I can see and feel their mood, even if you can't."

Johnny laughed harder and fell back toward the table. "They're worried it'll be hit, too. You don't have much of a line on my men. These are the sort to mourn the Gallow, not be afraid to pull into port."

"Tyrant's Gallow has a reputation both earned and unearned," Rone said. He sat with his arms crossed and looked at Charlotte. "I've never been there, but I've known enough travelers to tell you it isn't the place of debauchery and horror you always hear tales about."

"Oh, there's plenty of debauchery," Johnny said as smoke escaped his nostrils. "It's just not *all* hookers and opium."

Rone gave the captain an appraising look, then said to Charlotte. "There are, believe it or not, great merchant lords there, men who keep a good measure of control and order over the place." Rone said.

"Oh, those are the biggest villains of all." Johnny said. "Privateers have got nothing on the plays of the rich. And when you're talking rich privateers, ah, well…" He smiled and licked his lips. "That's a dangerous lot. But it's as good as place as any in the North Pelagian to find able hands. Probably a better place to find fellas who want to buy in, since we've had so many shares open up recently. Then we'll be on to Golice."

"Buy in?" Charlotte raised an eyebrow at Johnny.

"This is a private ship, deary," Johnny said. "A lot of those mutineers back in Masala were stockholders. Get paid by the ship's profits rather than a standard salary. Very lucrative for those trying to move up in the world, if a bit higher in risk."

"Who exactly owns this ship?" Charlotte asked.

"I own thirty-six percent. A goodly portion is owned by a wealthy trader in Golice, who fronted most of the capital for the purchase. The rest is – or was, rather – owned by the crew."

"So, when you joked and said you'd pay me a deck hand's wage, you meant you'd be signing over a portion of the ship's stock, right?" Rone asked.

"You already paid enough to buy out me and the rest of the crew. I could write you out some stock if you like, but will you be hanging around the Northmarch much to be collecting dividends, I wonder?"

"I may yet," Rone said. "I don't see myself going home."

"Veraland is home, eh?" Johnny said.

"I didn't say that."

"Yes, you did." The captain laughed.

*

Charlotte stood beside Rone as the tall, mountainous island grew larger, rising from the horizon as the ship sped on toward it. Eventually, the details of the kingless port of Tyrant's Gallow fell into place. The city was massive, surrounding a wide cove full of ships. On one side, cramped and stacked grey buildings went up a rolling mountainside, and on the other gleaming white cliffs backed towers and tile roofs, the tops of the city's mansions. From a distance, the city seemed well-planned, the whole thing designed to grow up the mountain which sheltered it, like a many-terraced castle. Long docks intersected the grid of the harbor, and dozens of ships, some flying colors and others without flags, floated there lazily.

"I must admit, it's other than I expected," Charlotte said.

"What did you expect?" Johnny said through a laugh. He was wearing a wrinkled brown jacket with tassels on the shoulders, and a shirt that was close to white. His large head and beard stuck out of the poorly-tailored clothes unflatteringly, and to Charlotte, he looked quite out of character.

"Are you planning on attending a state dinner?" Rone said.

Charlotte chuckled. "If drunken thieves have a king, maybe."

"Well, the Gallow can be a fancy sort of place, and I *am* trying to find some marines interested in stock options." Johnny tugged on his jacket. "Appearances can make or break a sale."

"I'm sure," Charlotte said. "You know, I must say this city is actually quite beautiful. I expected a decrepit pirate village, lawless and on fire."

"Oh, there's probably a few pirates here, lass, but burning buildings is generally bad for business, even for them. It's buildings that have all the loot, you know."

A splash erupted on the port side, followed by a cannon report. Charlotte flinched, and Rone instinctively reached for the pistol hidden in his jacket. "Are they shooting at us?" A bunker far in front of them had a puff of smoke coming from it.

"Relax, it's just to get our attention," Johnny said. He turned around and yelled, "Get the port colors out, white field!" Two men scrambled and started running a flag up the pulleys of the mast. The wind caught it near the top, and it shot out proud: two squares of blue and two squares of black set against a white field. Two small shots sounded over the water. "Excellent," Johnny said to Rone, "Our port of call isn't on the shit list."

"What happens if it is?" Rone asked.

"We fly a different flag." Johnny said.

"They already saw the first one, though."

Johnny shrugged. "I don't make the rules. I just follow them."

"Of course, you do," Rone said.

Johnny stepped away, giving orders to a few nearby men regarding the sails and the other riggings.

"What are you thinking?" Charlotte said, noticing Rone's

frown as he looked at the city. He nodded to a corner by the captain's quarters. She stepped into the shade with him.

"I'm wondering whether we stay on board or not," he said quietly. "I would normally say it would be safer to stay here, but…"

"You don't trust the captain."

"He's suffered on our account," Rone said. "There's no perfect option, as I expect that the fact that we are wanted on the Isle will be known here soon, if it isn't already. So, how do we hide from the eyes that are looking for us? Do we risk being in a place where we can't leave if they come looking? The crew here may be loyal to Johnny, but they're all pirates by my standards. I don't trust any of them."

"Well, then, we go ashore," Charlotte said.

Rone nodded. "Let's go pack. If we can leave with Johnny, we do so, if not, I'm sure we can find another ship to somewhere in the Northmarch, maybe even Hviterland itself."

II: The Gallow

he ship slowed as it approached a dock where a boy stood waiving a tall orange flag. Pierce and the other crew members threw the hawsers to a few shirtless dockhands as they closed the gap. They tied them down, and the Parkitees's crew began to pull the thick ropes back in, inching the ship closer to the dock until the hull made contact. Chains clanged as the anchor dropped and they set the gangplank down. Johnny strode down with an air of arrogance as a small bespectacled man wearing a tailored blue jacket and a matching set of pantaloons walked to the end of the dock. He was carrying a ledger and a pencil.

"Good afternoon, Mister, uh…" He looked up at Johnny.

"Johnny. Just Johnny."

"Very well, mister Just Johnny; my name is Reginald." He smiled as he extended his hand. Johnny shook it, narrowing his eyes. The little man ignored the expression and looked at his ledger. "The docking fee is six Argents, plus you owe an additional fifty-seven cyprals."

"What for, eh?"

"The cannonball and the powder to fire it. It's not our fault you forgot to fly your colors, mister Just Johnny." Without taking his eyes off the man, Johnny rustled around in the purse hanging from his belt and produced six large silver coins. They clinked as he dropped them in the little man's hand, who glanced at the varied sizes and heads effaced upon them with a smile.

"Ship name?"

"Parkitees." Johnny handed him a stack of large copper coins, equally unmatched in dimensions and design. Reginald weighed them casually before dropping them into his bag and withdrawing a handful of tiny copper cyprals.

"Excellent, sir. Can I ask the reason for your visit?"

"Oh," Johnny said, "Nothing to sell or deliver. We're here for minor re-supply and re-staffing."

"Very well, it should be fairly easy to find both. Mind that my dock is only for a week's stay at most. If you want to drop anchor for longer, you'll have to talk to someone else."

Johnny nodded to him and walked on, his hand on his long cutlass. Rone and Charlotte followed close behind him.

*

Gold Street was a long and rambling street, packed with enough people to make pulling a wagon through highly impractical. On each side, and often pushing into the common cobbled path, were awning-covered stands filled with merchants. The various types of goods seemed to be clustered together. Whether this was by decree or chance, Rone could not tell. Fishmongers were closest to the docks, along with net sellers, and as one walked further from the docks toward the motley center of town the stands began to be full of trade goods and tools, then finally finished products ready for sale. Clothing, tobacco, gunpowder, and even books liked tables near the central square of the city.

Eventually, they came to a wide thoroughfare where the paving stones of the street were at last visible amid the absence of a tightly packed crowd. They were a mottled white and gray, many old and weathered and many more newly cut, the result of a recent repair. Some of them were of granite and glittered in the mid-day sun like little jewels between darker cobbles of sandstone. The road forked; the narrower way went uphill to a procession of tightly packed buildings made of a mismatched assortment of materials and styles. Stone, brick, and wood houses with as many roofs and roof styles were clumped together. Several taller buildings jutted out like teeth in discolored gums above the line of homes on the hill.

"Here we are!" Johnny called back from a few paces in front of Rone and Charlotte.

Beyond him, the street opened up to a grand central square. Stone buildings lined the entire area, tall and imposing, with parapets and reinforced doors looking over the pavement. Charlotte's eyes widened at a dense complex of mansions that stretched up the mountain to the west. Many of the outlets of these buildings were coming directly out of a sandy white cliff, buttressed by masonry.

Johnny smiled and said, "I'm going to put up a few posts on the boards out here, then hit up the pubs and the slums. If you need anyone else from the crew, you know where to find 'em."

"The brothel?" Rone said.

"You bet!" Johnny said. "Or back on the ship once they've spent their tin." He walked up to a small wooden structure: three-sided with planks of wood covering its edifices. On all sides were nailed many sheets of paper. Most were advertisements for work or goods for sale. The gaps between these contained old words of graffiti, often carved into the wood. Some were mere statements: cryptic things like, "Fire moon piss," or the not-so-cryptic, "Janie's got the rot." Johnny began nailing up a sheet of paper that read:

*Hands needed on free-sailing vessel, mostly hauling, privateering contracts in effect (**freebooters welcome**). Inquire with the first mate or captain at the Parkitees on Dock twelve. Term pay, **Catch-and-prize pay in effect**. Stock buy-ins available (minority holdings only).*

"Alright," the captain said. "We'll have plenty signing up, I think."

"When will we be sailing?" Rone asked. "I don't want you leaving without us."

"Make sure you're back on board by dawn, the day after tomorrow. Keep in mind I have ways of finding you, at least in this ratty city, if you decide to skip out on me – I expect the other half of that payment."

Rone nodded. Johnny looked him over for a second, then smiled and strode away.

Rone turned to Charlotte, "Shall we find an inn, or would you prefer-"

"Yes," Charlotte interrupted. "I need a bath. So do you."

"When will that not be the case, I wonder?"

"When we set down somewhere civilized."

"What kind of lodgings do you want? Simple?" Rone pointed back the way they came. "civilized," he pointed up toward the stone mansions, "or queer?" He pointed off the way Johnny walked. The road was narrow and shaded, with crowded wooden buildings bending over the cobblestone walkway. It looked as though it wandered up to the old part of town crawling up the hill, with its mismatched assortment of homes and businesses.

"What's the point of wealth if you're going to spend it lodging with brigands and rogues?"

"Indeed." He looked down at her with a raised eyebrow, a slight smile on his lips.

"I didn't mean you."

"Of course," Rone said. He gestured for Charlotte to follow, and she did, grumbling softly to herself.

In the middle of the square, they encountered a great crowd. Most of the people there were simple-dressed merchants and other workers from the city. A few reeked of real wealth (literally – Rone choked on a whiff of strong perfume as he and Charlotte ambled around the crowd). As they walked the perimeter of the gathering, they could see what had garnered so much attention.

A raised wooden stage sat in the middle of the huge square, positioned to indirectly face an immense keep-like building on the west end of the open square, older and grimmer than the buildings about it. There were gallows in the middle of the stage, and stocks stood on two sides. A middle-aged bald man, portly and red-faced, his cloth looking expensive but neglected and dirty, kneeled with his head latched in a contraption very much approximating the stocks, but without hand-holes. Attached to the top of a tall frame was a blade, much like that of an ax. It was positioned to fall downward in an arc to the prisoner's neck.

A fat man wearing a large hat with a velvet robe and leggings that pinched his fat calves like sausage casings walked about the stage yelling to the crowd. A tall hooded man stood to one side near the execution device.

"Forty days!" the fat man said in a high, clear voice as the crowd jeered. "Forty days and the debt not paid. Not one Cypral, not even a seashell, was cast to his note holder for the principle, despite the contract!" He gestured at the bald man.

"What is that they've got him in?" Charlotte asked Rone in a hushed tone.

"It looks like a guillotine. It's considered humane in some places."

"Seems awful," she whispered.

"At least it looks sharp. Wouldn't want to just get half your head chopped off. Like getting tossed off a hooker half-way through a trick."

"That's disgusting," Charlotte said.

Rone chuckled softly. "If you don't laugh, you'll cry."

"It's still sick."

"Better this than what your husband does to criminals. Keep that in mind."

"Despite the guarantee of blood as collateral," the fat man on the stage continued yelling, "Despite this, he is unwilling to pay Madam Porthagan her proper due." The crowd chattered.

"I'm quite aware of all that," Charlotte whispered. "Don't make me think about it." She nodded toward the stage. "They are killing this man because he owes a debt?"

"That's what it seems like," Rone said. "Not unheard of in my line of work, though I've never seen it on display in public like this."

"However!" The fat man stopped and put his hand on his chest dramatically. "However!" he yelled again over the crowd, his voice cracking. "Madam Porthagan is not a cruel woman!" His frowned as numerous people in the assembly laughed loudly. His pitch began to rise, "She is not a woman without mercy! She is not a woman without compassion!" His voice calmed as the laughter subsided "She is merely a woman disinvested, a woman who, like any person, wishes to see her good-faith contracts fulfilled."

"Rubbish!" A man yelled loudly from the front row. "Mitha's making an example, nothing less."

The fat man on stage waved his hand in front of his face as if brushing the protestor off.

"Will anyone service this man's debt? The principle is high, very high, indeed!" The man stopped in front of the guillotine and leaned against it. "But the interest is low, so low."

"He'll never find a man to pay the principle. What's the point? Get on with it already; I came for a show!" A short fat woman shouted near the back of the crowd. A few tired laughs could be heard scattered throughout the gathering. The fat man went on like the woman hadn't spoken.

"A week's interest for a week of life, what do you say?"

"Yes, get on with it. I've wasted enough weeks listening to criers moan about it," another voice from the front rang out.

"Forty days his neck has been saved by the generosity of his fellows. Will this day be the end of Gallow's grace?" The man in the guillotine looked ragged, his beard unkempt, but he looked well-fed for having spent forty days in prison.

"Please don't!" A woman cried out from the front row. She was wearing a simple dress, which was worn and stained. Her brown hair fell greasy around her shoulders, streaked with a few strands of grey. She leaned up against the stage. "We will have the money, please!"

Rone grumbled and grabbed Charlotte's hand. "Let's get out of here. I don't want to watch this."

Charlotte resisted his pull. "You'd watch the execution, but a woman – probably that man's wife – asks for mercy, and you cringe? Some man you are."

Rone gritted his teeth. "I didn't *intend* to watch the execution either."

"How many wives have you left wailing like that?" Charlotte said, meeting Rone's eyes. He looked away quickly.

The fat man seemed not to notice the woman crying on the stage. "Perhaps today is the day after all. Ten argents!" He paused as if waiting for the crowd to gasp at this sum. "Will leave this man's head on another week. I ask again, will nobody service this man's debt?" He turned to look at a clock tower attached to the massive building behind him, the focus of the square, which read 11:59. "It seems with the end of silver, comes the end of time. In accordance with the customs of the Gold Courthouse, and in fulfillment of the terms written and stored with us, witnessed by three fellows and re-attested by a majority at the time of arrest, I proclaim the life of Mineo

Hergas Gordino the Younger to be forfeit as collateral of honest debt." He nodded to the hooded man, who had stood still and silent the entire time. He walked casually over to the execution device.

"Come on!" Rone hissed in Charlotte's ear.

"Wait!" Charlotte screamed, fighting against Rone's grip. The fat man held his hand up, and the executioner stopped in his tracks. "Wait! I will pay."

"Damnit, you foolish woman," Rone said in her ear, letting her drag him forward as he held onto her arm. "You don't know what you're getting into. You put your foot in this door, and you don't know if it will come out again."

She glanced at him, her eyes narrowed.

"Silver speaks, my good lady," the fat man said from the stage. Charlotte stormed forward and threw a handful of silver coins on the stage.

"I'll pay for next week, too," she said, looking up into the fat man's face with a hard gaze. The woman who had cried out before, busy pushing her way through the crowd at the front of the stage, finally reached Charlotte and began pawing her, thanking her through a stream of tears. Charlotte recoiled from the touch, pushing the woman's hands off her and feeling suddenly very exposed as she saw the whole crowd staring.

"I'm afraid that according to the contract we cannot accept payment for interest not accrued. And alas," he began a bow, "the principle must be paid in full or not at all in the case of a third party, as the agreement requires a one-hundred percent buyout. It is all in the contract, and as a mere arbiter of such, it is out of my power. So sorry." There was a false genuineness to his words, like a well-trained actor performing one of the old dramas.

"Come off it! You just want a job for next week!" someone jeered from the crowd. Laughter erupted.

The crier stepped forward, ignoring the jeers, and smiled at the crowd. "I'm afraid there shall be no bloodshed today, beloved fellows, dukes and dames." The masked man removed the wooden stocks of the guillotine and then he pulled Mineo up by his hands, which were bound behind him, before handing the prisoner off to a nearby man at arms. The temporarily relieved prisoner looked in Charlotte's eyes and nodded before he was forced to stumble down the steps. The crowd began grumbling audibly.

"Let us hope this doesn't bog us down," Rone whispered tersely in her ear. "We can't afford to dally picking up pebbles."

"This isn't a pebble; it's a man's life!" Charlotte whispered back.

"Fear not, we shall have a treat for our honored witnesses!" The fat mat pulled a watermelon from a burlap sack sitting nearby. He began fixing the wooden stocks of the guillotine around it.

"All men's lives are but pebbles in the path of great men," Rone whispered.

"Well, I'm picking this one up," Charlotte said.

"Let's hope it doesn't give the wolves an opportunity to catch our scent." Rone's eyes were searching around the perimeter of the square, taking in the faces there.

The fat man pulled a rope and the crowd cheered as the blade of the guillotine swung down and sliced the watermelon in two. He tossed the halves into the mass of people, who began passing them around, taking out a small piece of the melon each to eat.

"Tomorrow shall be a packed day in the Gallow square, my compatriots!" he cried. "Eleven in the morning shall toll an auction of thrall, recently acquired pirates no less, and some of them are lovely young women! Help your fellows recoup their losses and acquire some help for yourself at the same time!"

The fat man bowed low and a few people clapped. He gathered up the silver coins, still sitting on the stage, and tucked them into a purse hanging at his belt. As he walked off the side of the stage, he looked over at Charlotte and scowled, the pleasant façade of master of ceremonies discarded like a melon rind.

"How could you just sit there and watch a man die?" Charlotte said to Rone. Her eyes searched over his blank face.

"I *wouldn't* have chosen to watch. We did nothing to bring about that man's situation, and it looks like there will be nothing we can do to remedy it permanently. I don't like to witness the ill-fate of others, but I also know we had no part in bringing it about."

"Please, you have to help us," the woman who had cried out earlier said. Rone and Charlotte turned their attention to her as she ran her hands, which were grey from some kind of dirty work, over Charlotte. "And thank you, I can't thank you enough." Rone looked at Charlotte with a crinkle in his brow, as if saying to her without words, *I told you so.*

"It was… nothing," Charlotte stammered, looking noticeably uncomfortable, "Miss...?"

"Martelena Gordino- Mineo is my husband," tears were still streaming down her face. She began to say something else, but the words stopped in her gullet when Rone, looking hard into her eyes, held a finger up to his mouth. He nodded to the side of the stage.

They turned to look where Rone was gazing, and they saw an ostentatious woman staring at them from the back of a rickshaw on the other side of the square. Her make-up was thick and colorful, and around her neck hung a highly decorative jeweled necklace, glittering in the sun. Her dress, blood red, glinted in a thousand places as its neat pleats folded down and obscured her legs. A tight corset pushed her bosom up, displaying the pale white assets given to women of leisure.

The rickshaw she sat in was no less baroque. Stiff silk details and plush velvet cushions lined the inside in a bright blue. The outside was a labyrinth of ornate carving. She put a fan up over her face, tightening her gaze on Rone, who stared back like a statue.

"Who is that?" he said.

"Mitha Porthagan," Martelena said flatly. They watched as she barked an order at two shirtless grey-skinned men who were very muscular and who possessed the yellow eyes particular to the eastern race, who began to pull her rickshaw away.

"Why doesn't she have a horse and carriage?" Charlotte asked.

"Anyone can own a horse," Rone said. The rickshaw moved off, going north up the broad avenue to the cliffs.

"My husband – lazy bastard though he is – has done nothing but right for that shrew Mitha, and she's going to take his head," Martelena said as she turned back to face them. "Ship sunk within sight of port while Mineo was doing what she demanded him do. She's bloodthirsty. All I need is a few more days, just a few days to sell our stocks in Nantien – we have piles after all the years in the business – and then we can pay her back in full."

"Nantien?" Rone.

"Yes, there's a customs house there that deals with Divine Strand stocks."

Rone took a deep breath and shared a silent look with Charlotte. "Good luck," Rone began in a polite tone. "We've got to get going. I hope everything turns out for you." Rone grabbed Charlotte's hand and she finally allowed herself to be dragged off.

"Wait!" the woman cried out, but Rone had already disappeared with Charlotte into the dispersing crowd.

III: No Strangers

Rone and Charlotte found a room in a place called the Bowling Inn, an orderly and clean establishment that had been designed to impress, though clearly by someone not of the aristocracy. Rather than marble tiles, it had polished floorboards. The tables and bar, well-carved and polished deeply, were of durable maple rather than an exotic hardwood. The ceiling was decorated with clouds but was too low for a house of elevated manners. These details by themselves were neither vices nor virtues, but the owner and barkeep (a middle-aged man named Dathis with receding hair who wore a simple well-laundered apron) priced his accommodations well-above what they should have fetched. As a result, his establishment was almost entirely vacant.

Rone considered it an appropriate choice as soon as Charlotte pointed these things out, and so he hired a room over her complaints. They spent the night there, much as they had before, with Rone asleep on his bedroll by the room's fireplace, facing the door.

"Do you ever get tired of being on edge?" she asked him once she had put out the lamp, and the shutters of the window were closed against the moon. "Always facing doors and looking into shadows?"

"It's normal for me. Don't worry about it. It's what you hired me for."

"That's not what I asked. I asked if you grew tired of it. Aren't you exhausted from it all?"

Rone was silent for a moment. "Yes, but I don't know if I

could ever be different. All the things I've done... the messes I've been in..." He sighed. "I don't even know how many enemies I have out there."

"I'm sorry."

"I thought I was settled-in at Cataling, but it seems I just cannot turn down an adventure."

"Well, you have certainly taken me on one of those."

Rone chuckled. "Let's get some sleep."

"It should be easy, now that my bed isn't rocking back and forth."

"A hard floor or a moving mattress... hard to know which is better."

Charlotte waited a few moments, then said quietly. "It's a big bed. I won't even know you're here."

Rone didn't answer. When Charlotte woke in the morning, he was already up sitting by the open window, looking out a narrow gap in the shutters. She reached over and felt the sheets next to her, and thought maybe they had been disturbed.

At Rone's demand, they spent the entire day indoors. Charlotte whittled the time away by attempting to read from the sparse library of the inn, comprised mainly of travel memoirs and older novels which held no interest for her. Rone spent his time in the room carefully attending to his weapons. His blades seemed to have picked up flecks of rust from the sea air, and he grumbled about it as he worked them out with a smooth white whetstone.

That afternoon they dined alone on a roasted chicken in the corner of the common room after each of them had enjoyed a hot bath.

"You know," Charlotte said, holding up a piece of the chicken on a silver fork, "this is a fair bit better than that wild rabbit, but not nearly as much as I expected."

"Are you insulting my cooking, or theirs?" Rone said, frowning above a smirk.

Charlotte smiled back. "I was merely pontificating that in the context of all the bad food we've had, I expected a good meal to be a more satisfying experience."

"So, it's *my* food that was bad."

"Alright grumps, you take that how you like it."

"The rabbits *were* a bit sage-y, but good fare for how hungry we were, I thought."

"Yes, hunger," Charlotte said. "But I am finding, however odd, that a fair environment does not enhance the meal experience as much as being hungry. How about that?"

"A little less insulting. Maybe I should let you cook our rabbits from now on."

Charlotte shrugged. "I never learned how to cook. Sorry. Not necessary for someone like me."

"I thought you were from the country. You shoot like it. Do they teach you to shoot but not to eat what you kill?"

Charlotte chuckled. "Eat it, perhaps, but not cook it. Sometimes we just gave the kill away. Hunting is a past-time. Only peasants hunt for food."

"Thanks," Rone said.

"It's not an insult. My point is, I still can't cook. I can make tea, but that's about it."

"I shall continue providing full service, then."

Rone flinched and jumped out of his chair, his hand going to his pistol, though he didn't draw it from its place within his jacket. Charlotte turned and saw Mitha Porthagan had entered the dining room, accompanied by two men armed with long guns. She wore a smirk on her face and held up a gentle hand to Rone. Behind her, the sun was in the west, and the edges of her silhouette seemed to sparkle.

She calmly approached the table, the pleats of her dress

(blue that day) lifted slightly to reveal her shoes and ankles. As the door closed and the typical window light returned, Charlotte gave a small gasp. The glinting of the dress was from many tiny pearls and cut gemstones, each dangling by a filigree sewn into the satin fabric of her dress.

"May I join you?" she said in a clear, mellow voice. She didn't wait for a response. Instead, she gestured to one of her men, who quickly brought another chair to the table. She sat and stared at Charlotte, her eyes half-lidded. Charlotte frowned and stared back, taking in the lines of the woman's face, subtle around her mouth and eyes.

Mitha broke the stare to catch the eye of the innkeeper. "Wine."

Dathis nodded curtly and disappeared to a storeroom.

Mitha turned back and looked at Rone, who was still standing, his body poised for action. "Who are you?"

"I'm Halbara, and this is my husband-" Charlotte began, but stopped at a smirk from Mitha and a wave of her hand.

"No, no. I know who *you* are," Mitha said. "I have a portrait of you in my sitting room, Charlotte. I've seen that huge portrait of you in Frostmouth at least a half dozen times, too, though I prefer *my* painting as it better captures your innocence. Darus Roth always did his best iterations of you in the smaller formats. No, what I want to know is," she turned her eyes on Rone, "who is this man you have with you? And you can sit down, of course. If intended to kill you, I wouldn't risk being here myself."

Charlotte drew a blank as Rone sat down, his hand still inside his jacket. "This is… my husband…" she stammered, not wanting to speak the truth and not knowing how she should lie.

Mitha laughed. "You're not married. Even if I didn't know who you were, I would know you two aren't married. Your manners say you are noble, and you show far too much affection for your companion for him to be your husband. Nobles never marry for love. Perhaps he's your lover? Affairs make wonderful stories. And here you are, with no Sarthius Cattannel. Very interesting."

Charlotte opened her mouth to speak, but could not seem to conjure any words, which was just as well, for Dathis had returned with a set of glasses and a few dusty bottles of wine.

"So," he said, setting out the glasses on the table. "I have this bottle, which is three argents. It's a-"

"Do I look like a woman who cares about the price of a wine bottle?" Mitha said, raising her eyebrows at the innkeeper.

"Of course not," Dathis stammered. "I'll just, er…" He put the bottles down and picked one of them back up. He began working the cork out with a screw awkwardly as Mitha stared at him. It came out with a pop, and he began to fill the glasses. When they were all half-filled, he walked away with the spare bottles under his arm.

Mitha picked up a glass and took a sip. She made a face and called back to Dathis, "This port is meant to be watered down."

Dathis turned back. "Oh… yes of course. Let me just…" He dashed back toward the bar.

Mitha sighed. "At least it's a decent vintage from Rhonia." She swirled the nearly black wine around in the glass, watching it coat the freshly cleaned crystal.

The innkeeper returned and poured a small amount of water in each glass. Mitha nodded curtly, dismissing him. She turned her eyes back to Rone, who was looking at his wine glass in an almost accusatory way.

"You were about to tell me who you were."

Rone spoke, "I'm an agent of fortune."

"That's *what* you are, not *who* you are," Mitha said.

"I am who my employer needs me to be," Rone said.

"I see," Mitha said. "Who is your employer?"

"Not you," Rone said.

Mitha looked at Charlotte for a fleeting second and smirked. "Not her."

Rone twitched his eyebrow. "Her."

"You're a bad card player, sir," Mitha said. She touched her lips in thought. "What rumors do wash up on these shores… which ones shall I believe?"

"Whichever ones suit you," Rone said.

"How do you know Mineo?"

"Who?" Charlotte said, trying to place the name.

"The man from the stocks," Mitha said, raising an eyebrow.

"Um… We don't," Charlotte said, "I just… pitied him. I didn't see why he should die when just a few silver could save him."

"For today. Mineo has very little goodwill left here. Even those who pity him will eventually find their hearts heavy, but their purses much too light. Mineo is not a particularly wicked man, just a foolish one, and one who tends to be as foolish with other people's property as he is with his own. He sank a very fine ship of mine trying to run a blockade, something beyond the scope of his job and his skill as a seaman."

"Why would you not let us pay for a few more days of interest?" Charlotte felt a bit of flush on her neck as she watched the woman across from her continue to stare blankly back.

"The courthouse keeps its rules, and I keep mine. If they won't accept payment, that is their concern."

"Can we pay you directly?" Charlotte asked.

"I don't know why you would. There would be no record

of it. Mineo could still be hanged next week, not that I would see to it. Giving an individual money for a debt in the public bank is generally unwise here."

"So, you are saying that you are not to be trusted with a few silver?" Charlotte said.

"A few silver is a fortune to the right people, you know."

"But to you, I can see it is not a fortune," Charlotte said. "And yet you cannot be trusted with it."

Mithu snorted softly. "Darling, I don't make a habit of trusting people without something at stake to back it up, and neither should you. And I came here for business, not flaccid insults. That should be beneath one such as you."

Mitha stood up and turned to the two armed men, who sat at a nearby table whispering. With a nod, they stood and walked back to the door.

"But I think we are not in business together just yet. Be careful whose toes you step on whilst in Tyrant's Gallow. Titles mean very, very little here, Charlotte. I look forward to our next meeting – when you are more polite."

Mitha followed her guards out the door, to where a lavish Rickshaw awaited her.

Rone stood up and said. "Let's get packing."

Charlotte nodded and stood up with him.

"Not going to second guess me?" Rone said.

"Not this time," Charlotte said. "That woman is a stomach-turner for sure. And she knows Darus Roth, which is like having the carpet pulled out from under you."

"Darus Roth?" Rone said as he walked toward the stairs.

"A… friend from when I was a child. A painter. He was employed as a house artist by my uncle, Vegard."

Rone paused on the stairs and looked back. "The King of Hviterland?"

"Didn't you know that?" Charlotte said.

"I never really kept tabs on the extended families of the elite, nor did I care too deeply to know whom Sarthius married. Originally, at least."

"Any idea where we should head?"

"To find Johnny and hopefully get off this island," Rone said. "If he hasn't already left."

"What makes you think he has?"

Rone grumbled in response.

*

They found Johnny in the third, and ugliest, pub Rone and Charlotte popped into – a dank affair called "Regget's." Johnny, due to his great height, was someone that the other innkeepers and casual drinkers had paid attention to, and so his trail for the day was easy to pick up. He was likewise easy to spot when they finally caught up to him in the crowded, dingy bar that was as dark as night inside, despite it being afternoon outside. His great hairy head stuck up from a group of bow-legged sailors like he was surrounded by children, and his face was beet red from drinking. The low hanging wooden rafters, looking near collapse due to dry rot and countless holes of unknown cause, made Johnny look more the giant he was, especially as he leaned his head this way and that to avoid hitting them. The pub's furnishings were equally neglected, made of mismatched tables and chairs, chipped glasses and plates, and nubby candles left naked on wood countertops. The floor was covered with sawdust, and Charlotte could see why, as an old woman retched in a far corner while a young man slapped her on the back.

"Dreamer, what kind of crew is he trying to hire here?" Charlotte said quietly to Rone.

"Pirates, methinks," Rone said. "Wait here."

Charlotte nodded and pushed herself against a wooden pillar beside two young and very drunk men arguing over which whore had the prettiest nipples. In other circumstances, she would have laughed, but the reeking, oppressive atmosphere of the inn made her humorless. She tried to ignore the men and watched Rone slide sideways through the milling crowd.

She clutched at her jacket and reached for the pistol Rone had given her as the crowd suddenly began pushing her backward until she pressed into the two men discussing the finer points of female anatomy for hire. Charlotte was shorter than most of the people in the pub, and she immediately lost track of Rone. She craned her neck up, trying to see what was going on as the people continued to jostle each other. The drunk men laughed as they stumbled backward.

Not knowing what else to do, she dropped to a squat and inched between the tightly-packed legs, half crawling toward where sunlight had fallen on the dust-littered floor. Heavy boots walked past her. She stood up suddenly, knocking a beer out a man's hand (who quickly quieted his temper when he caught her face), as she saw a group of armed men confronting Johnny. At their head was none other than Vindrel, the man who had pursued her since her escape from Cataling.

Charlotte choked and covered her mouth.

"What's the meaning of this?" Johnny said as two men laid hands on him, one of them holding a stout set of iron cuffs. Another man stood at attention nearby, his hand on a scabbarded sword. Johnny threw one of the men backward with a single, great arm, then used that same arm to strike the man holding the sword in the face, knocking him back into the crowd of bystanders. He then flopped onto Vindrel, taking the last man who was still holding him down with him. His fists moved wildly over Vindrel, and Charlotte saw that he got in several hearty blows before the recovered attackers seized him again. He froze as two armored men moved up beside him with raised muskets.

"As an officer of the Gold Courthouse, I am authorized and bound to take you into temporary custody to keep the peace," said the man with his hand on his sword, who was dusting himself off.

"I've done nothing against custom or law," Johnny said.

"Not here, tis true, sir," the officer said. "Other than assaulting officers of the court. We have an extradition request. Is this him?" The officer turned to regard Vindrel, who was pushing himself up with one hand, as the other was in a sling. His face was already swelling, and blood dripped from his nose.

His eyes slid over Charlotte for just a moment as one of the nearby men helped him up. The glance was enough to make her skin crawl, and she took a step back instinctively. He seemed particularly strong for a man she had shot just a fortnight past, and even Johnny's heavy blows had not suppressed his energy.

"That's him," Vindrel said, wiping blood from his mouth. "The king of Veraland demands his justice."

"Vindrel," Johnny said. He laughed and said with a slurring drawl, "He's no officer of the government. He's a bloody dream-worshipper. A sell-sword. A sorcerer, too! The king of the Green Isle is dead, damn it."

Vindrel smiled at him darkly.

The officer's voice remained even. "We'll sort it all out if that's the case. We've never turned a man over for political reasons, but we don't like to harbor criminals, either. Come with me, Mister Johnny."

Charlotte watched Johnny, now with his wrists in irons, get pulled toward the door. Their eyes met for a moment, and he frowned at her. Vindrel turned to look at the scowl, but before he could, Charlotte felt herself being pulled down toward the ground. Between the legs of two men, Charlotte watched Vindrel scan the crowd curiously before walking to the door, looking stiff but otherwise well.

It had been Rone who pulled her down. He met her eyes and kept a touched a finger to her lips. She nodded.

Slowly, the people in the tavern spread back out, conversation returning to old topics or the exciting new incident. Laughter erupted in many places.

"Shit," Rone said, helping Charlotte back up.

"The Gallow never lacks for entertainment!" said a young man, one of the ones Charlotte recognized from the earlier unsavory conversation. He slapped Rone on the shoulder and gave him a wide smile that lacked front teeth.

"Indeed, but it's best not to be part of it. Remember that, friend," Rone said, and shook the man's shoulder. The man laughed and held up a flagon, but Rone shrugged as he had no drink. The lad began to guzzle his own, and a few voices around them cheered.

Rone pulled Charlotte further away, then whispered, "This is very bad."

"So much for outrunning anyone," Charlotte said.

"You're right, and let's not panic. It won't be as bad this time," Rone said. He sighed and ran his fingers through his hair. "Vindrel doesn't have any political advantage in this port. Johnny may even be freed within the week."

"By that time, won't they find us?"

"I'm not waiting around a week to find out," Rone said. "We'll start looking for something that can get us out discreetly at dawn."

"What about Johnny?"

"What about him?" Rone said. "He's either locked up for a time or sent back to the Isle; either way, he can't help us now."

"Rone, we can't just leave him, after all that he did for us,"

Charlotte said.

"I think we'll have to. This isn't the kind of business where nobody eats a loss because of risk."

"But the loss of life," Charlotte said. "That's really different. Johnny could be executed."

"So could I, if we're caught. You'll just go back."

"Back?" Charlotte said. "Oh, Rone, if only you knew… I might prefer execution."

"Then we have to get out of here as soon as possible. I'm very sorry about Johnny." Rone reached out and grasped her hand, squeezing it and locking eyes with her. "We'll wait here just a little while; then we need to hurry to… whoever has all the ships' registrations."

She inched closer to him, and he put his arm lightly around her. After what felt like a long stretch, he retrieved their packs and led her out the door.

It was late afternoon. The sun dipping behind the western hills, and the clouds moving above them were already painted in shades of pale orange.

"We'd best be quick. If that central square doesn't have the ship registrations, the dock houses will have an idea who is going where," Rone said, mostly to himself. "This is just my fortune."

"Johnny's is a fair bit worse. Don't forget," Charlotte said, almost running to keep up with Rone's long strides.

"You're right, of course, but it's my luck that will hang him."

Rone stopped short, halting Charlotte with an extended arm. "Hold up." He nodded. Straight ahead, in the large square, was a gathering of armed men. They were dressed like those that arrested Johnny, and they were talking amongst themselves in a relaxed sort of way, leaning against the now empty stage.

"Here," Rone said and pulled Charlotte between two open shop tables. The shade from the west was deepening. Rone looked down and began fingering a few bolts of cloth on one of the tables.

"No discounts for the end of the day," the fat shopkeeper said from the large chair where he sat reading a book.

"Bulk?" Rone said, glancing at him, then back to where the men were gathering.

"Of course."

"What do you think, dear?" Rone said, nudging Charlotte.

"Oh," Charlotte said, tearing her eyes from the armed men and looking down at the cloth bolts. "Let me think about what we need."

A silent few moments passed.

"I don't think I see anything I want."

"I have more inside," the shopkeeper said, again not moving his eyes from his reading material.

"We have to go, I'm afraid," Rone said. "Thank you."

The fat man grunted in response, then Rone pulled Charlotte away and to one of the narrower streets that lead down to the docks.

"I could just barely hear them," Rone quietly said as they walked. "They were talking about trying to find us, I think. Luckily they didn't seem to want to try very hard."

They paused near a little alleyway that pointed straight down toward the cove and harbor.

"That might be a dock house down there," Rone said, pointing to a low bunker-like building on the edge of the water. A few men armed with pikes were standing nearby it, relaxed. "But that's a no-go, right now."

"What should we do?"

Rone looked around. "Let's find somewhere to be for a while. A room at an inn, maybe. I'll think of something."

"I know you will," Charlotte said. "I trust you to. But just to re-assure me – am I wrong to think these local men at arms aren't very concerned?"

"You're not wrong, but Vindrel is here. I don't know how he caught up to us, but he did. Again. Luckily I can guess how he'll work – always above ground, and as you said, these locals don't seem to care."

"Let's get moving, then," Charlotte said.

Rone nodded.

IV: Lords of Legend

They took a turn past the bar where Johnny had been mobbed, into an area of town that was very between things – it was between clean and dirty, old and new, and predictable and queer. Rone found a boarding house there that had a few vacancies, including an entire room. It had no common space, and thus there were few eyes to take note of them. The owner, an old widow, seemed to care little about them besides warning them that the front door would be locked shortly after the evening bells.

When they got to their room, Rone appraised himself in a mirror. "I should have gotten to a barber," he said, feeling his beard.

"I like the beard," Charlotte said, sitting on the bed, watching the sun go down outside the window. She had a book in her arms that she had neglected to return from the bowling inn, but she was uninterested in reading it. "I can scarcely remember you clean-shaven."

"We should cut and die your hair, too," Rone said, turning to look at her.

"You've threatened that before."

"Yes, and I was stupid to think we were out of it." He sighed. "I can probably shave myself if I had a good bit of soap."

"I have a good bit of soap," Charlotte said. She got up and rummaged in one of the bags for a minute, then produced a small, misshapen piece of yellow soap. "But won't Vindrel recognize you more easily clean-shaven?"

"I'm sure he would, but it's more to avoid the guard. I'm assuming he merely described us."

"He doesn't know what I look like," Charlotte said. "He looked right at me in the bar but did nothing. It gave me an awful shiver."

"Thank the dreamer he didn't catch sight of *me*."

Charlotte stood up and stood beside Rone by the mirror. "We look like nobody special," she said, smiling slightly. "My hair even looks brown with these brown clothes."

"Me, maybe, but you... You'll always stand out. Real, true beauty always draws the eye." Rone turned and looked at her.

She gazed up at him with an almost expectant openness to her eyes. "You said you were weak to a pretty face. Did you really mean that, or were you just trying to be charming?"

"I didn't mean it," Rone said. "Pretty isn't strong enough a word. Pretty is a serving woman with slender arms and yellow hair. You?" He shook his head. "Something else entirely. Something I can't properly describe. I'm no poet."

Charlotte smiled and, to Rone's surprise, a few tears dripped from the corners of her eyes. "Thank you." She reached forward and touched his arms. "You've been cold."

"I mean to be. I'm afraid to look at you." Rone found that he was holding both of her arms, right below her shoulders. Impulsively, he closed his eyes to the blue rings of fire that were hers and kissed her lightly on the lips. He lingered for a moment, then pulled back. "I'm afraid I'll lose control."

"Maybe it's okay to."

"No, it's not right. I have dreams about you. I..." He took a steadying breath and released her.

"I have dreams about you, too," Charlotte said. "But you already knew that. Please, Rone, just tell me-"

She stopped at a knock at the door.

"Who is it?" Rone said, motioning toward his pistol.

Charlotte retrieved it from the table quickly.

"Name's Horace," came a voice, muffled by the door.

"I don't know a Horace. You must have the wrong room."

"Rone, right?"

Rone growled softly.

"Just a message for you, sir. Or for Charlotte, rather. I don't-"

"From whom?"

"The Lady Mitha Porthagan, sir."

"Twice?" Charlotte said, stepping back toward the bed to find her own pistol.

"Quiet," Rone said.

"Well," said Horus from the other side of the door. "If you need me to come back, I suppose I can, but, uh…"

A folded letter appeared from beneath the door. Charlotte bent down and retrieved it. It was sealed along one of its edges with wax, stamped with an anchor emblem.

"That's the message. I'll come back in a minute to fetch you, yeah?"

"Fetch us?" Rone said. Giving in to an impulse, he unlocked the door, quickly threw it open, and grabbed the collar of the man who stood outside. The young stranger was tall, matching Rone's height, but was perhaps half as heavy, with narrow shoulders that made his jacket look awkwardly generous on his frame. He smiled nervously and held up empty hands as Rone dragged him inside, his pistol pointed to the lad's chest.

"Why are you here?" Rone said. "We already talked to Porthagan."

"She told me not to promise nothing, but I think she can keep the courthouse from finding you. They're looking for you, right? Anyway, you're invited to dinner, only nobody is supposed to see you coming."

Rone shook his head. Charlotte began opening the letter.

"You really think I'm not going to shoot you?" Rone said.

Horus smiled awkwardly. "I don't think Mitha would be sending me into danger, sir. I mean, look at me!" He gave a forced laugh.

Rone smiled at him. "Fine," he said and eased down the hammer of his pistol. He put it back in his jacket but kept one hand on his backsword, which still hung at his hip.

"It's a very kindly-worded dinner invitation," Charlotte said, reading through the letter. "Except it implies that if we don't come, something bad will happen to us." Charlotte looked at the paper again. "Here. 'I would hate to see you suffer because you didn't choose the right company. Dinner will be late for you, but my servants will be disappointed if you aren't able to attend.' Does that mean this boy will kill us if we don't go?"

Horus shook his head nervously as Rone drew his sword out a few inches. "No, no," he said, holding up his hands. "I just find people. That's it! And she just means the cook. He'll be disappointed. He loves his job, and-"

"This last bit," Charlotte said. "'I'm sorry more of your party can't join us.' She must know about Johnny already."

"The pirate, yeah. Come on," Horus said. "I can take you up a back way."

"How did you find us?" Rone said.

Horus smiled. "Well, I just asked around. That and I showed the right people the picture. Here." He withdrew a folded piece of paper from his baggy black jacket and opened it up. Inside were two charcoal drawings, slightly smudged, showing Charlotte and Rone in accurate detail. "Mitha got it from someone or other. Do you think she'll be mad I smudged it a bit?"

"Does the guard have a copy of that?" Rone said.

"Which guard?" Horus chuckled. "If you mean the Courthouse guards, then no, I don't think so. They'll be coming round soon, though. My buddy Teller words for the Gold Courthouse, and they'll be pressing their privilege to find the fugitives. That's why Mitha told me to find you straight away."

"Right, very kind of her." Rone scratched at his beard. "Mitha has ships, right?"

"A handful, yeah, but she owns stock in loads more," Horus said.

"You're not thinking of meeting with her, are you?" Charlotte said.

"She could get us off of this island," Rone said. "She found us easily enough, though I don't know who could have drawn that picture. If she wanted to ransom you, we'd likely already be fighting. And I believe that the guard will start going door to door if they're working for Vindrel."

"I'll follow you, Rone, but I don't trust her," Charlotte said.

"I don't trust her as a person, but she could be made to see the advantage of helping you. In fact, I'm sure she already does. I'll risk it. Take us, Horus."

*

The last traces of dusk had left the horizon by the time they had packed and followed Horus out of the back door of the boarding house, once again not bothering to tell the keeper of the house they had left. The narrow alleyway the thin young man led them through quickly deepened to a colorless gloom as the sky overhead turned from pale orange to deep blue. The sun, waxing, was already in the sky, providing scant silver light as they went.

"This way," Horus said, pausing at an over-large wrought-iron garden gate. Ivy covered the old brick walls, but it was all well-trimmed. Beyond the gate was what looked like a wood crawling right up to the city. He took out a large iron key and fit it into a lock, one of half a dozen linked together to keep the gate shut. They went in, and Horus closed the gate behind them, latching the lock through the iron bars.

"What sort of garden is this?" Charlotte asked as they walked into the darkened canopy of trees. Within a few steps, the night deepened and it looked as though they were in an ancient forest of menacing blackness.

"It's not a garden, it's the hunting grounds," Horus replied. "Mitha and a few of the other lords maintain it for their amusement. They even have deer and foxes shipped in for the hunt." He drew from somewhere in his baggy jacket a small lamp. It sprang to life in his hands of its own accord, illuminating the space around them in many hues before settling into a warm orange.

"How did you do that?" Rone said.

Horus smiled at him, and his thin face looked strangely inhuman in the lamplight. "What do you mean?"

"You have the spark," Rone said.

Horus shrugged. "Just a spark, though."

"That's a rare talent, lad. What my father wouldn't give to see it again, even if it is merely a spark."

"Was he a wizard? A real one?"

"No, just a spark, like you, but he forgot, somehow. It was a pain on his heart unto his death, that loss. I never understood it."

"I'd heard that Tyrant's Gallow was a city of wizards, and here we are," Charlotte said. "Walking next to one."

"Not a wizard," Horus said with a chuckle. "I can light a lamp. There are a few others around that can, too. The Church doesn't hold much sway around here, so you see it from time to time." He chuckled and paused at a stone marker on the path. There was a fork just past it. "Look over there."

A short way up the path was a wall and a small gatehouse, complete with a portcullis. An ominous and ancient stone building rose behind it, topped with a parapet and alight in many windows.

"That one belongs to Seamus Delving, in case you ever wanted to have lunch with the terror of the south sea." He glanced back at them, "He actually loves guests. He's quite the character. Tells excellent jokes. This end of the city is full of people like that if you know where to look. Lots of sailors retire here because they can buy a nice property. Nobody gives them guff about where they got their loot if they have enough of it."

"Was the city always lawless?" Charlotte asked.

"We're not lawless, miss," Horus said. "We *are* kingless, but not lawless."

"Have you ever had a king? Who wrote the laws?" Charlotte said.

"You don't need a king to write laws," Horus said. "All the laws we need, we have anyways, so why worry about a king now? Men like Delving keep it orderly enough."

"There are no kings in the mountains either," Rone said. "At least, we recognize no kingship, whatever the lowlanders say. We still have laws. The old code. It's better than a king, in my opinion."

Horus waved them forward, along the other fork, back into the strangely artificial forest.

"Now, as to whether we've ever *had* a king," he said at length. "As far as records can go, there's never been one, though the city was occupied a few times in the last thousand years or so. There is a legend if you like to hear it."

"Of course," Charlotte said.

"Well, the story that gets told around here says that many, many years ago there was a king in Tyrant's Gallow, only it wasn't called Tyrant's Gallow back then, it was called Convection because the King's family name was Convect. Anyway, this king supposedly lived in a gold palace. He was also known to consort with wizards. The island became a gathering place of sorts for them because of his tolerant attitude and our distance from the mainland."

"And now it's a gathering place for pirate princes," Charlotte said.

"Begging your pardon, but we don't tolerate pirates. Privateers, freebooters…" Horus laughed to himself, "they're a different sort. "Madam Porthagan has put out quite a few bounties on people stupid enough to prey on her ships, and it's called the Gallow for more reasons than the tyrant."

"Which you were getting to, I assume," Charlotte said.

Horus nodded. "Eventually the Church of the Twelve heard about the lavish King Convect and his cabal of dark wizards, and raised an army to put a stop to it. This was supposedly back before the start of the sixth Dominion, which meant guns and cannons were yet to be, um…"

"Canonized?" Charlotte said.

Horus laughed. "That's a good one. Yeah, there were no cannons back then, so the church couldn't just send a fleet to sit in the harbor and blast the place to smithereens. Some tales differ, but supposedly the whole affair was actually the work of the king's older half-brother, who couldn't take the throne because he was a bastard. He was supposedly angry about being forced to join the clergy and live a life of poverty."

"Poverty? Hardly." Rone laughed. "When was the last time you stepped into a church?"

"Never have, actually," Horus replied. They turned another corner and saw the end of the wood. A stone wall greeted them, and beyond it, lit by the pale moon, was the high and famous Gallow Bluffs, mottled white and grey in the night.

Dots of orange light littered the cliffside above the steeples of large houses, their fronts obscured by the wall that marked the end of the lavish hunting grounds.

"Can't fault you for that," Rone said.

"This story was a long time ago," Horus said. "Maybe the church wasn't quite so rich back then."

"Once, the church taught magic, if you go back far enough. Would you believe it?"

"Yeah, I would," Horus said. "But that ain't the church in this story. The church has no real army, you know, so what really happened was an invasion by a few of the lords of the Petty Kingdoms and the Lowlands, all gone or forgotten by now, of course. The invasion force was overwhelming, but they were repelled from the harbor by the power of the wizards. They still had access to magic back then, even though it was long after the sundering of the dream-"

"Wait," Charlotte said. "Sundering of the dream?"

"When the Fay, the eternal dream, was lost to the waking world," Rone said. "And with it, the flows of the prim dried up and were lost. Magic was lost. Or almost so."

"What are you talking about?" Charlotte said.

Rone smiled to himself. "I forget sometimes."

"Forget what?" Charlotte said.

"How sheltered you were." Rone watched Charlotte frown at him. "I'll tell you the stories of the ancient world - the true history of Midgard – some other time. Or do you believe that the twelve are the beginning and ending?"

Ignoring the question, Charlotte said, "Go on, Horus."

"Yar. The wizards still had magic, and they also had many inventions they had come to develop over long years of tolerance. For ten days, the wizards fought, and many of the invading force's ships were burned. The quest was on the verge of abandonment by the parties involved, who each held a deep distrust of the other.

"One night, the king's brother, who had orchestrated the whole thing, took a single boat and rowed up to a beach outside the city. He was arrested by the king's guards but was taken to see his brother once his true identity was learned. Everyone thought he had arrived to give the king strategic information, and at first, he feigned to give it, but at the same time, he secretly poisoned the king's wine. The king was found dead the next day."

"So, the brother became king?" Charlotte asked.

"Yes, that's exactly what happened. The king's advisor notified him that, as the last surviving member of the Convect family, the crown had fallen to him, bastard or no. The advisor gave him the king's crown and clothed him in lavish robes. Servants trimmed his hair and beard. The new king was now prepared to end hostilities with the crippled fleet, but before he could even leave the palace, the admirals of the attacking force and a high priest walked in the front doors of the castle. They had found the streets empty and the wizards' machines unmanned. No guards were posted outside the palace gate. The brother, who now resembled the old king in appearance, was put in chains and dragged outside the palace.

"They hanged him there for high apostasy in front of the mixed armies of the petty lords in an otherwise deserted street. The palace was searched, and a writ of succession was found, naming 'Fontaine' to be the next legal heir to the king, should no blood relative be found. The high cleric declared it legal and stamped it. Soon it was discovered, by virtue of a lone soldier that had traveled here before, that 'Fontaine' was merely the mountain on the island. Needless to say, that man earned an ugly fate for his honesty. Frustrated by the king's will, and unable to come to a consensus on who should rule the island, the petty princes began to argue with one another.

Violence broke out, and many of the armed men who came ashore died. The last prince, victorious and standing in the town square on a hill of dead men, declared himself king.

"At that time, the king's advisor approached. The petty prince soon found himself surrounded by the city's wizards, who stood on balconies and atop buildings that rung the square. They were armed with their staves, guns, and other mechanical death devices. They destroyed the prince's remaining force with their magic, ending the lives of the invading soldiers in seconds. The advisor then declared the prince a criminal, and the wizards hanged him beside the new king. The advisor sent a courier to the Hand of the Divine with the high cleric's stamped writ. After that, the island officially became ruled by the mountain. In essence, free to itself. Of course, it's probably all nonsense, and there have been other conquests since. I think we're just a hard lot to rule."

"What happened to the king's advisor?" Charlotte asked.

"He was a wise wizard and had the golden palace rebuilt into the golden courthouse, of which he became the first chairman," Horus said. "The gold from the bricks and decor of the king was melted down and used as the monetary base for a new bank in the same place. It's all legend though- even the Golden Courthouse's records have gaps and limitations due to fire and things like that. Ah, we're here."

V: The Golden Palace

They came to another wall with another iron gate, though this one had fewer locks holding the heavy chain in place. Beyond it was a wide paved street winding downhill to their right and disappearing to their left in a tangle of tall, stately buildings. On the other side of the road was something well beyond words like "estate" or "manor." It was the real golden palace of Tyrant's Gallow, a vast complex made to look like a castle, if not function as one, and though it was now night, the moonlight gathered on the structures which were all just as white as the light.

A stone wall of light-colored stone stood some twenty feet high, and the narrow parapet at the top was defended a few feet below by a row of iron barbs pointed outward. The outlet at the center was held by a double iron portcullis topped by machicolations and, Rone assumed, by a murder hole hidden between the gates. A guard armed with a musket watched them from a window in the small gatehouse.

Behind the wall, the manor itself climbed *into* the cliff behind it. Above the end of the masonry, balconies emerged from the stone itself, carved into the living rock. All of them held inner lights, and a few of them had above them small portholes from shafts cut into the rock to carry off smoke.

"This is incredible," Rone said, pausing to stare up at the high places of the mansion.

"It's been here a long time, but it wasn't quite as nice when she got her hands on it," Horus said as he made two swift gestures to the guard in the gatehouse. The guard got up stiffly, and after a few moments, the first gate ascended to allow them passage. The trio stepped into the arch, and Rone looked up to see a large circle of black iron that sealed off the murder hole. "Evening, Bart," Horus said to the grate.

"Hullo, Horus. Mind the paint in the second hallway, some of it is fresh," the man said, bowing slightly at Rone and Charlotte as he lowered the first gate back.

"Will do," Horus said. The second gate opened, and the pair walked through into a wide and well-tended courtyard. Low hedges, alive with small yellow blossoms all closing in the cool evening, lined the walkway to either side as they walked. Two white horses stood far off to one side, lazily browsing at a trough near an open stable. Blossoming trees stood near the far walls on either side, their colors muted by the night. Following Horus, Charlotte and Rone walked up the steps toward a massive set of reinforced doors covered with bas-relief.

What had first appeared to be carvings upon the doors turned out up-close to be hammered steel with a dull-colored luster in places. Large and dense, the door rang out with a deep groaning tone when Horus used the knocker, which hung from a large metal dragon head set into the right door. It had a match on the other side, and when taken as one piece, the bodies of two dragons emanated from the knockers, wings splayed wide to the arched stone door frame. Their claws clutched at the earth, and each tail crossed into the other door, eventually resting on its mate. The dragons also had a pale green hue in the raised steel, just noticeable in the lamplight. Rone mused on the color – the artist must have placed copper there before pounding the sheet of iron into its delicate shape. Despite the tension of the moment, he smiled as he regarded the artistry.

A peep-hole, unnoticed previously, suddenly opened up,

revealing a set of brown eyes. A voice spoke, "Oh, it's you, Horus. Dinner will be ready soon. Those the guests?"

"They are," Horus said. The sliding of metal sounded from the other side of the door. After a moment, the door began to move inward, grinding at first over the sparse dust on the floor, then moving silently once it was well clear of the door frame. The house steward, a squat, older man with dark brown skin, dressed in a red jacket, was pulling on a circular handle as large around as his head, straining against the weight of it.

"You gonna show them up for me?" he asked with a strained voice. "She's up in the drawing-room. The high one."

"I might as well. Wouldn't want to interrupt your nap, Nom." Horus was smiling.

"It's my knees, not my eyes. You'll get old one day too, lad," the steward said.

"Only if I'm lucky. This way, friends." Horus motioned them out of the low antechamber. The hall they stepped into was almost oppressive in its magnificence, built more like a temple than a home. Pristine white floors, made of carefully fit together marble slabs with no grout, polished to a shine, filled the hall, and ran out to rooms unseen. Moonlight illuminated arched stained-glass windows reaching twenty feet above them, going into what in a typical mansion would be the second story. The combination of the many lamps in the hall and the moonlight beyond made their colors strangely bright. Rone stared at one off to his left, showing the god Ferral over his forge, which burned with red and yellow glass. In the next window over was his sister (and wife, depending on the book) Artifia, at work at a potter's wheel. As he looked around the high-walled receiving room, he saw all twelve gods arranged in their calendar order after Artifia, all the way to Verbus, the god of death and poetry, at the very end of the hall.

Rone was surprised that the merchant baron did not have

a particularly exalted place for Denarthal, the god of money. He was more surprised to see the dragons painted along the walls to either side of them as they walked out of the entrance hall and into a narrower gallery. No less detailed than the front door, the gallery walls were covered with frescoes of wyrms in carefully layered paint that sparkled with some inner mineral as Horus's lamp swung in front of him. Some of the beasts were in flight, others stood upon mountains and castles, and some breathed fire of gilt paint. At the end of the gallery was a dragon examining a book, resting in a comfortable chair. The paint glistened on the curing plaster, still slightly wet.

Rone paused and stared at it.

"I rather like that new one," Horus said, holding up his lamp to the wall. "Makes me smile. Just a bit of silliness, having a dragon reading – not Mitha's usual taste."

"I don't think there's anything silly about it," Rone said. "There's a lot of symbolism in dragons, and my guess is they can read as well as you and me."

"I can't read very well," Horus said. He chuckled. "If only they were real, eh?"

"Perhaps they *were* real, once," Rone said. "Maybe they will be again, eh?"

Horus shrugged and motioned them onward.

He made more small talk as they walked down other hallways and climbed several small staircases, always moving up and further from the front door. Eventually, they reached a spiral staircase and began ascending. The stairwell started to feel small and stuffy as they walked up, and Charlotte and Rone realized that there were no longer any windows. Charlotte put her hand out and touched the cold wall, detecting no seams for stones.

"Yes, these stairs are carved out of the living rock. Quite a feat, isn't it?" Horus said. "Nobody knows how they did it so well. One of the lost arts, maybe."

As he spoke, they reached a landing, and Horus pulled open a carved wooden door. It opened up into a large room floored with a smooth white tile. Plush carpets sat beneath ornate furniture, which was arranged around a fire in a small hearth. At the end of the long room, red curtains blocked off a balcony. As the curtains flapped in the breeze, they saw the silhouette of a woman sitting in a large chair, and beyond her was sky, moon, and clouds.

On the wall hung a few paintings; one of these Rone paused at to stare. Charlotte at first did not notice he stopped moving, but her heart leapt, and she nearly choked aloud when she turned back to him. On the wall above an ornate couch was a small portrait of herself.

"It looks just like you," Rone said. "*Is* it you?"

Charlotte felt her voice stick. "It's the painting she mentioned," she said with an effort. "It's from another life." She grabbed at Rone's sleeve and pulled him onward.

Horus walked forward and stood outside the balcony, then cleared his throat.

"As requested, madam, here are the guests."

"Thank you, Horus," Mitha said as she stood up.

"Thank you," Charlotte said, smiling and nodding slightly to Horus. The messenger turned around and took a stack of paper from Mitha as she presented it to him.

"These are the paychecks for the week," Mitha said. "You can leave the night guard's in the desk in the foyer. If you could tomorrow, take the stubs to the office and pick up this week's cleared checks from the Gold House." Mitha turned to Charlotte and Rone. "Welcome to my humble abode." She extended her hand. Charlotte shook it daintily. When she presented it to Rone, he awkwardly followed suit. Her hand felt soft and well cared for, but he sensed a strength and tightness in the tendons, even as it sat lightly across his fingers, that was dissonant with her delicate image. Mitha raised her eyebrow and cracked a sardonic smirk as Rone held her hand. "I have some hot tea," she continued, "Won't you sit and have some with me? Dinner will be ready soon, and I am sure that you will find it satisfying."

"I'd rather get down to business," Rone said. "You own a good deal of ships, and stock in-"

"Not yet. We'll get there, I'm sure, but not yet. Tea first, and conversation."

"It would be a pleasure," Charlotte said flatly after a short silence.

Mitha cracked a slight smile as she turned away from them.

They followed her past the flowing red curtains to the balcony, which was a jutting section of the cliff that had been carved into a semi-circular sitting area. Even the banisters were made of living rock, polished smooth and only lightly worn by the wind and rain. A cool breeze blew across the stone, and from there, they could see the entire city Tyrant's Gallow stretching out below them as a haphazard web of lights, flowing down the hill to the mouth of the river and the harbor. Countless ships stood amid the docks with hundreds of tiny lights on them.

The height dizzied Charlotte slightly, and she leaned on Rone for support until she found herself sitting in one of the large blue upholstered chairs that sat near the rail. Rone sat beside her in an identical chair. He made to cross his legs but stopped at a quick gesture of Charlotte's hand over his lap. Mitha set herself down in a green chair that faced the other two.

Near at hand was an easel with a half-finished painting upon it, depicting the moon over a night harbor. On a nearby table were a tea set and a hot kettle. Mitha leaned back, making no effort to pour the tea.

"Will you pour me a cup, dear?" Charlotte said.

Rone gave her a curious look but complied.

"Me too," Mitha said. She smiled as Rone handed her a cup and a saucer.

"I see that you paint," Charlotte said.

"A hobby of mine. It's good to cultivate one's artistic senses."

"Judging by your hallways, they are very refined, even impressive."

"Having money helps. One day I would like to take a more direct hand in some of the decorating, but as you can see, my skills are not yet up to my standards."

"When your standards are as high as what you have on display, you must be gentle with yourself," Charlotte said, sipping the tea. "You have only been studying for… what, five years?"

"Two," Mitha said. "But I appreciate the compliment. I wish I had more time for it. Have you studied art or merely sat for it?"

"Darus Roth was my teacher, actually," Charlotte said. "I didn't have much talent for it, I think. My talent was music."

"I thought you said you were bad at it," Rone said.

"I said that I was bad at the cello," Charlotte said. "I was far better at singing and at the harpsichord, too, despite my small hands."

"I should be so lucky as to study with Darus, regardless of my talents."

"I don't think you'd be saying that in my place."

"Why is that?" Mitha said. "Is it because Darus was in love with you, or are you saying that because of something unrelated in your life, like being forced to marry that snake

Sarthius?"

"Hold on," Rone said, leaning forward. "I don't care who you are; you can't talk to her that way."

Mitha smiled at him. "Rone… You're reaching for your gun. The fact that I didn't have you disarmed was a gesture you apparently did not understand."

Rone clenched his jaw.

"And were you really offended I called Catannel a snake? Charlotte's husband is quite contemptible, or would you not be extracting her from her marriage so vigorously?"

Rone leaned back down.

Mitha relaxed as well, then touched something at her leg, under the folds of her skirts: a slight, unmistakable bulge. Rone nodded at the gesture.

"I should have guessed a pirate would have a pistol hidden."

"Symmetry, my boy," Mitha said. "That's how you do proper business, but I get ahead of myself." She looked at Charlotte. "Was I wrong to assume he loved you?"

Charlotte was silent for a few moments. "No."

"You can see it so clearly in his work. It's such an ideal representation, slavishly perfect." She looked out to the night. "It must have been torture for him, looking at you all the time, but never getting to have you. And it must have been uncomfortable for you, too." She glanced back at Rone, then back out to the harbor. She sighed. "You are indeed very interesting, Charlotte, and you keep interesting company. Pirates, assassins, and spies… You would make a good queen."

Charlotte rubbed her temples. "I just want to go home."

Mitha's face warmed slightly as she looked back at Charlotte. "I know. I think it's time to dine. I'll escort you." Mitha stood up and straightened her skirts. "Rone, be a dear, and hold our lamp."

Rone frowned at her, but at a concerned look from Charlotte, obeyed. They followed Mitha into the room and back to the stairs, with Rone holding the lamp aloft for light. When they reached the bottom, she took them through another well-decorated gallery.

"How did you know my name?" Rone said. "When you sent Horus for us? And where did you procure a sketch of us?"

"All in due time, my boy," Mitha said.

Eventually, they descended another short, straight set of stairs and came to a set of reinforced doors. They were painted with wreaths of flowers, but otherwise straight and plain.

Beyond the doors was the night above a large candle-lit dining table near to a roaring open cook pit. Nearby, a young woman was playing softly at a large clavichord. The piece was gentle and introspective, with a sweet, ornamented melody above a slow bass line. Sitting around the table were several men who were busy sipping wine but stood up when they noticed Mitha stepping down into the dining area.

"Glad you all could make it," Mitha said. She turned her head toward the cook pit. "How long, Marty?"

An old, tall man turned up his head, revealing yellow eyes and sallow, grey skin – the trademarks of Draesen heritage. He smiled and said, "About two minutes to finish cooking, just to get the crust right, then another two minutes to carve up." He moved over to a spit and turned over a rack of meat that was nearly sitting on the coals.

Mitha looked back at Rone, who had one hand in his jacket, gripping his pistol. The other rested on the hilt of his backsword.

"It's alright, my friend." One of the men from the table stepped away, closer to a lamp hanging from a nearby post. He had blonde hair and a tight beard along with a bandage around his neck.

"Farthow," Rone said. "I did not expect to see you here."

"I didn't expect to be here," he said, smiling. "But alas, our mutual friend Drath Harec felt it prudent to have me accompany the great expedition of the Veraland navy. I arrived this afternoon with Vindrel."

"You could have warned us," Rone said.

"I'm sorry I couldn't manage it. Vindrel took a gamble, and I suppose it worked out for him, though not for your friend."

"There's more at stake than an unlucky privateer," Mitha said. "Have a seat, please."

"I came here hoping to hire a ship," Rone said.

"We'll get to that," Mitha said. "Please don't offend my cook by refusing to dine." She nodded toward two empty seats, near her own.

Charlotte stepped around Rone and went to one of the chairs, leaving her bodyguard to follow her. Farthow slapped Rone on the shoulder and took his seat next to him.

"Allow me to introduce you all to Charlotte and Rone," Mitha said.

"Your reputation precedes you," a dark-skinned, grey-haired man said, nodding between Farthow and Rone.

"This is Seamus Delving, a friend and a party that has a knack for knowing the interesting things that happen in this town."

"The terror of the Datala Sea," Rone said.

"Depends on who you talk to," Seamus said. "These days I mostly like to hunt and have wine with interesting people. But interesting times have a way of calling me into action."

Mitha gestured to another man. "This is my chief associate, Teal Starnly."

"Pleased to meet you," a lean, middle-aged man said.

Rone nodded to him and finally seated himself next to Charlotte.

"And here we are," Mitha said. "The wife of Sarthius Catannel, the future king of Veraland, and niece of Vegard of Hviterland, in our confidence."

"And," Charlotte paused and thought for a moment, "What do you need from me?"

"From you? Nothing, really, but we can do much *for* you. Like I said, business."

Charlotte looked at her hands, then back at Mitha. "I'm hesitant to do business with someone who executes her partners."

Delving chuckled but didn't speak.

"You mean Mineo?" Mitha sighed and leaned forward. "Many people would wish him dead in my position. He took a merchant ship I bought for him and sank it trying to run a blockade. Still, I don't really wish him to be *dead*. The truth is, I don't care whether he lives or dies; he's just a bad business partner. Unfortunately, having a soft heart attracts men like that. I enforce the contract for the sake of all the others, not because I hate Mineo."

Mitha smiled as the grey-skinned cook brought over the roast. He plopped it on a platter and began carving it. He served Mitha first, putting the thin-sliced meat on her plate along with some vegetables from a nearby pot.

"The sea's a rough business," Delving said. "Your friend Johnny understands."

"I daresay he does," Rone said. "Since he's sitting in prison, I presume."

"I was thinking of him killing his first mate. Farthow told me the story. Quite impressive. I've dealt with mutiny before – always with death. No room for mercy out on the blue. Thank you," Delving said as the cook piled meat on his plate.

"I can't argue with that. So what is this business you have in mind?"

"Your escape from the Veraland navy, of course," Mitha said.

Rone chuckled. "So, you have a ship?"

"Not one that can carry you," Mitha said. "Farthow brings word that the rest of the fleet will be attempting to block up the port by dawn. Apparently, they were delayed in Nantien."

"Admiral Dunneal decided to stop and establish dominion in Nantien," Farthow said. "Observing that it had just been sacked, but the attacking force was gone."

"Reprehensible," Rone said.

"Sensible," Delving said. "It's' what I would have done if I were him. Nantien is a rich port."

"But the Draesen leave anything worth plundering?"

"The Draesenith Empire?" Mitha said, dropping her fork. "In the North Pelagian? You must jest."

Rone shrugged. "It was them. I'm sure."

"They're going to invade somewhere in the Northmarch," Charlotte said. "They have expeditions every twenty years or so, over the Frostbacks or across the tundra during the summer melt. It's about time."

"But why did the Draesen abandon it after sacking it?" Rone said. "I figured they were looking for a strategic stronghold."

"Interesting supposition," Starnly said, rubbing his face. "Very interesting. It makes sense, though. Nantien was just a raid for supplies, then. It has no strategic use in any part of the Northmarch."

"We'll have to worry about that wild card later," Mitha said. "For now, know that I cannot spare a ship to run through a blockade against a navy so well equipped as what the Green Isle has sent. Instead, what I propose is that you take the Parkitees."

"We can't," Rone said. He ignored the fresh food on his

plate. "Johnny is locked up. His crew is loyal to him. Or are you proposing we steal his ship?" He shook his head. "Don't answer that. I won't steal a man's ship, especially one who has paid so much for us already."

"I can provide the staff," Mitha said. "I can also ensure that you get past the warships, at least initially. We know a few ways to sail out of here that our opponents will not."

"We also are not planning on stealing it," said Starnly. "We'll acquire the appropriate share in stock to control it."

"Buy the stock? From whom? Johnny?" Rone said.

"Precisely."

"He'll work with us," Mitha said. "Mister Delving and I have deep connections at the courthouse, and Starnly is the best solicitor in the city. We'll be able to keep him out of the hands of Veraland indefinitely."

"We might be able to get him released when it's said and done," Starnly said. "It may take a while, but it'll be worth a good share in the ship."

"Surely you have enough ships already," Rone said.

"I'm not in the business of charity," Mitha said. "Truthfully, it's more trouble than what I will gain in a small-time private vessel. I'm more interested in keeping Charlotte out of the hands of Sarthius Catannel. A kingless Veraland is an attractive business opportunity."

"For us all," Delving said.

"The stock in the ship is in the interest of symmetry," Mitha said. "We have to all have risk and responsibility – toward each other."

"Also, my boy," Delving said, looking at Rone, "you must remember that Johnny has a crew that is not locked up. They deserve their freedom, too, yes?"

"What happens to Johnny in the meantime?" Rone said.

Delving shrugged. "The Gold Courthouse is very kind to

prisoners."

Rone shook his head. "Vindrel won't leave Johnny behind."

"He will when he realizes you have slipped away and are heading east," Mitha said.

"You don't know him as well as I do. He won't let it go. He'll stay, or else come back swiftly to settle things."

"Do you have a better plan?" Farthow said. "Because this a rather good one."

"All I ask in addition," Mitha said. "Is a promissory note from the lady Charlotte toward King Vegard, her uncle."

"Of what quantity?" Charlotte said. "I can pay directly."

"It's not money I want," Mitha said. "I merely want a letter that states you are in my social debt and are thankful for me helping you."

"What good would that do?" Rone said.

"A great deal, at the right time," Mitha said. "Do we have a deal?"

Rone took a breath and looked at Charlotte intensely. "It's as good as we're likely to get."

Charlotte took a breath. "When do we leave, sunrise?"

"I'm afraid not," Mitha said. "It'll have to be tomorrow night, as we've already missed the right tide to skip outside of the blockade. You'll be taking the ship along a narrow channel, past a shallow island outside of the port. You'll hit bottom at any other tide. The sailors whom Mister Starnly will select will be able to navigate it without trouble."

"That's another day for them to catch up with us," Rone said.

Farthow laughed. "They've already caught you, Mister Stonefield. It's time for another escape. You're an expert at it, at this point."

"You can stay here tonight and tomorrow," Mitha said.

"This Cataling captain won't be able to find you within the manor."

"Very well," Rone said. "It's a deal." He nodded toward Charlotte. "I assume she knows what to write."

She looked at her hands folded in her lap for a few moments, then said, "Alright. I'll write a nice letter for you, Miss Porthagan, but don't expect my uncle to care about it."

"I expect he will care a great deal," Mitha said. Once again, she looked at Rone, her narrowed eyes communicating some hidden intent about which Charlotte could only guess. "But if he doesn't, then it hasn't cost you much, has it?"

"I suppose not."

"Splendid. Now then, since most of our business is concluded, our keyboardist has a proper set of repertoire for us to enjoy. Unless you are too tired?"

Charlotte shook her head.

Mitha smiled. "Rone, would you and Farthow re-convey the details you have on the sacking of Nantien to Mister Starnly? I'm sure he'll need it in the coming weeks. A fleet of Eastern warships is a significant hazard. And I promise you won't have to miss much of the concert."

"I'll need to be going, actually," Farthow said. "My superiors on this outing will be wanting my professional advice."

VI: Entries and Episodes

The fingers of the harpsichordist blurred as she executed each flourish. She liked to hold her fingertips up mid-air before the end of each phrase, letting the penultimate chord fully speak its expectant tension before she gave the cadence its due. The movement she played was slow and somber, with but a single, highly ornamented melody and a bold set of chords in the bass range. Her brow wrinkled and she squeezed her mouth during the most active sections, letting her whole body express the dark mood of this, the middle movement of her own sonata. At last, she played a final mordent and cadenced on a broad minor chord. She let the chord breathe a few seconds in the resonate hall, lined from floor to ceiling with unfinished maple, then began the next movement.

It started with a single melody, fast, yet sorrowful. The melody entered again, transposed into an even darker mode while the first voice countered it with a series of dramatic leaps. The melody entered a third and a fourth time as the dense fugue exposed itself. The harpsichordist's face fell to a lineless relaxed beauty in her total concentration. Only her dark eyes revealed what a high price the music demanded of her.

Charlotte felt oddly comfortable watching the concert. The Harpsichordist had bowed and begun to play the ornate gilded device as soon as Charlotte sat down. She and Mitha were alone during the first notes but were quickly joined by Nom, the steward, and Marty, the cook, who sat down in incidental chairs at the back of the hall. The purity of the musician's presentation had a way of blunting the tension she felt sitting next to the brooding Mitha Porthagan.

As the fugue went on, Charlotte tracked the voices as they wove into one another in episodes of harmony and strife, occasionally breaking out in an entry of the opening subject.

"Marvelous, isn't she?" Mitha said quietly. "Her name is Joseala. She is the daughter of a freighter captain that worked for me who was lost at sea. I took pity on her and decided to pay for an education. It turns out she has quite the facility in music, as you can see."

Charlotte thought back to her own musical education experience. Her mother had been a gifted singer, she remembered, and Charlotte was encouraged to develop her voice, but her father considered a woman singing in public to be improper for a lady. Even her aptitude at the keyboard had been suppressed, and her father had forbidden her to perform in public. For the wealthy, the arts were past times; entertainment was to be hired from the middle classes.

Mitha interrupted Charlotte's thoughts again. "I was thinking of having her tour the mainland; get her some exposure. If she doesn't find some career opportunities, she might at least find a nice husband."

"Yes, she is a natural talent, and beautiful too," Charlotte said.

"So, she's got at least two things people want. I hope she finds something she wants in return." They listened to the music for a few seconds before Mitha said. "Your bodyguard."

"What about him?"

Mitha made a wordless sound, then said, "How good is he?"

"He's gotten me this far," Charlotte said. "And to me, that is a feat. Just getting me out of Cataling was a feat."

Mitha watched the harpsichordist and smiled slightly. "I think I might like to take him to bed with me tonight if that's all right with you."

"What?" Charlotte said, loud enough that the girl on stage missed a note and hesitated mid-phrase. "What did you just say?"

Mitha turned to her calmly. "I figured he has missed out on a great deal of comfort."

"No," Charlotte said. She noticed the keyboardist looking at her askance.

"No, he has hasn't missed out on sex, or no, you won't let me sleep with him?" Mitha touched her lips. "Maybe it's not your decision to make. I'll invite him up for a glass of brandy-"

"No... Just no!" Charlotte said, leaning forward with a frown.

"What if I made a trade?" Mitha said. "You let me keep your bodyguard, I send you off to Hviterland on one of my ships?"

"I can't believe..." Charlotte felt sweat bursting on her brow. She stood up over Mitha and grabbed her skirt with her fists. "And I thought you were trying to be noble!" On stage, Joseala paused and started a technical passage over again.

"I am noble, technically, and this is quite how they act," Mitha said calmly. "Which makes me wonder about you." Seeing Charlotte turn to go, Mitha reached out a hand and grabbed her arm. "Relax, girl."

Charlotte turned back to see her frowning and looking genuinely sad.

"Forgive me. I sometimes push too hard, playing my games. Please sit down."

Charlotte slowly sat back down. They watched Joseala finish her piece and clapped as she stood up and bowed. She sat back down and began a somber allemande.

"You know," Mitha said. "You can't hold onto your feelings, even if he feels the same for you, which he doesn't."

"He does," Charlotte said.

"You know it?"

Charlotte remained silent and continued to watch the performance.

"You know very well what he is," Mitha said.

"He's a hero."

"He's a *killer*."

"Just a matter of perspective, as my uncle would say."

"Vegard is a shrewd man. But I tell you, people don't change. You should see him as he is. He's a spy. An assassin. A *murderer*."

"I can only judge him as I see him. He's a good man."

"To *you*, he is, for now. I can put you on a ship within the next fortnight to take you all the way to Frostmouth. You can leave him behind. He's served his purpose. I see how hard a time you have standing up to him."

"Maybe," Charlotte said. "And maybe I'm not willing to cast people off like broken tools once they have filled their purpose."

"You'd best learn to. Catannel is cunning, or else your peril would be less."

"He's evil."

"All the worse, my dear. I pity you."

*

There was a soft knock at the door. Charlotte raised her hands from her hands, wiping tears from her cheeks, which began to feel hot with embarrassment.

"Who is it?" she called at the door, glancing at the nearly full moon in the window. How long had she been missing? She remembered a full moon from sometime in the dry highlands east of Cataling.

"It's Rone."

She suddenly remembered what Rone had made her do in Masala, and she fumbled a pistol out of her bag, spilling part of the prime as she tried to catch it.

She cursed softly to herself and pushed her cheeks to her shoulders, trying to dry them as she walked to the door. She slid back the bolt and open the door a crack, saw Rone's face dimly in the hallway. She opened the door all the way and lowered the pistol.

"Good of you to remember your defenses," he said.

"Where were you?"

"Had a bit of a talk with Starnly, about the crew, just trying to plan ahead for a few things. Nothing you need to worry about."

He stepped in, then shut the door behind him and locked it.

"Mitha had another room prepared for you," Charlotte said.

Rone gave her a puzzled look.

"You don't have to stay in here," Charlotte said.

"Do you feel safe here?"

"Yes. Do you?"

"I never feel safe. Or maybe I should say, safe compared to what?"

"I don't know."

Rone frowned. "Then I guess I don't know either."

Charlotte sighed with exacerbation. "Just go. I'll keep the door latched tight till morning."

Rone frowned again, and the flickering lamplight distorted his features, making him look older and more tired. He nodded and reached inside his jacket. He withdrew a letter and handed it to Charlotte.

"Farthow?" Charlotte said. Rone nodded. She opened the

envelope and read:

To the ugly stone man:

Slipped away from my spouse again. Had to write you a letter, my love.

The Big Man will have to be at a hearing tomorrow at eleven bells. He'll be heading home with Vafty for sure. Sorry I couldn't get to him first. Was looking for you in the wrong place.

Rest of the wooden crew inbound, maybe here the day after tomorrow for a good party, so Missy's idea is nice, except Vafty is trying to get a hold of the Big Man's rowboat. It's in the pound with the other dogs, luckily. No manners, that one.

I'll be throwing my hat into court tomorrow for the Big Man's sake. I don't think it will work.

Might be nice to find another ship for your coca.

-B

"I don't think I understand this," Charlotte said.

"Johnny's ship is impounded, and Vindrel is trying to get at it. He's got a hearing tomorrow at 11 AM, after which he'll be handed over. Sorry, Charlotte," Rone said. He looked out the window at the moon and scratched his chin.

"What option do we have?"

"Try to contract a ship from Mitha, or someone else, at great expense," Rone said. "Mitha won't have anything leaving for a few days, which will be a problem if the fleet gets any bigger, or, if I guess correctly, they start a conflict. If we try to find somebody else's ship, we could end up traveling with a criminal."

"A worse one, you mean," Charlotte said.

Rone chuckled awkwardly. "Should we get to work on that?"

Charlotte shook her head. "No. I'm not ready to throw our captain to the wolves after what he went through with us."

"That's not under our control," Rone said.

"I have something in mind."

"What is it?"

Charlotte stood up and half-smiled. "I'll tell you tomorrow."

"Why tomorrow?"

"So that you can't avoid it."

Rone shook his head. "No. Charlotte, we're moving on."

"That's my prerogative."

"You hired me to get you home safely. I intend to fulfill at least *that* part of my contract."

"Good," Charlotte said. "But you still work for me. And I'm not leaving a friend to die on my account. Not again."

"What do you mean?"

"Ardala," Charlotte said. She held her smirk, but her eyes were trembling. Tears were filling her lower lids.

"You don't know what happened to her," Rone said. "She's probably fine."

"Don't lie to yourself, Rone. You worked for Sarthius. You know what he does to traitors or those of whom he even suspects betrayal."

"We cannot undo what we have done," Rone said. "We have to keep moving, otherwise Ardala… her death will be in vain."

"What death is not in vain?" Charlotte said. "And we are already walking back into the past, don't you see? Taking me home… I can't un-marry Sarthius, Rone. I can't undo what he did to me… but I can find again some part of the peace I once had, even if all my dreams are dead and blown away like blossoms at the passing of spring. I have no illusions of a life without regrets. I don't think you do either, but I know if I have a chance of avoiding regret in the now, I will take it over trying to walk back into the past once again."

"I've already learned that you can't walk back into the past, Charlotte."

"Your people are dying. Mine are very much alive." Charlotte paused. She walked to the bed and sat down on the edge of it. Rone sat down beside her and leaned over, putting his elbows onto his knees, hanging his head.

"You were an assassin," Charlotte said.

"Among other things," Rone said. "You hadn't figured that out by now? You've seen me kill."

"Why didn't you tell me what you did before?" Charlotte said.

"You never asked."

"I guess I wanted to believe other things."

"Like what? I was just a rustic who wanted adventure?"

"That you were a good man."

Rone looked at her askance. "I wanted to be a good man. I wanted to be a good man again. I thought by helping you, I could… redeem myself. But here I am doing it all over again. I'm a criminal again."

"I thought the Somnietel lived by their own code."

"I broke the code."

Charlotte laid her hand on Rone's arm. "You decided to do a good thing for me."

"Men have died in the process of doing good for you," Rone said. "And Ardala, too, if we are being honest. And I *should* be honest and stop being such a liar. I don't see how I can be a good man like this."

Charlotte leaned over and kissed Rone on the cheek. "I think maybe you should stop worrying about being good and just be what I need you to be."

"And what do you need me to be?"

"My hero." With that, Charlotte wrapped her arms around Rone and began to weep in earnest. "I need you to save me, Rone."

Rone touched her face and lifted it toward his. He forced a smile. "You're not making it easy, you know."

Charlotte smiled through the tears. "I probably never will make it easy on you."

Rone shrugged. "Keeps life interesting."

Charlotte laid her head on Rone's shoulder, and he hesitantly wrapped an arm around her. She looked at the moon. "You know, you never asked me what it was like."

"What?"

"Being Sarthius's wife. You never asked what it was like."

"I figured you would tell me if you needed to. If it was important."

"You're lying again, Rone."

"Shit. Well, I suppose I didn't want to know. I'd rather write my own story for you."

"Still?"

"No," Rone said. "Tell me your story."

Charlotte paused and locked eyes with Rone for a moment. "How much choice have you had in your life?"

"A great deal," Rone said. "Not that I've made the most of that freedom."

"As a woman, I have no choice. Maybe peasant women can decide things for themselves, but the nobility?" She shook her head. "I think peasant girls dream of pretty weddings to hansom princes. I always knew that was a foolish fantasy. My parents didn't have a very happy marriage. My father was the brother of the king, and he had choice – he got to choose my mother. She didn't get to choose him.

"When I think about her now, I still remember her as the most beautiful woman on earth, with shining blue eyes and hair that was golden-brown; she was from Latheria, and looked so different than all of my relatives: shorter, but more elegant. I can see why my father chose her.

"You mean she looked like you," Rone said. "Minus the hair."

Charlotte smiled. "Thank you for that. She was miserable – not used to life in the country where my father's estates were. We traveled to see my uncle in Vargana, which is a busy and beautiful port, as often as my father would allow it. So, from an early age, I could see that my life would probably be similar – married to an ill-tempered man who I wouldn't know beforehand.

"So it was I ended up betrothed to Sarthius Catannel. We had only met once before our wedding, and it was when he stopped by our estate for other business. He seemed utterly disinterested in me at first. He caught me when he was leaving wrestling with one of my brothers behind the stable. I remember he gave me this strange, ugly smile. I hated it."

"I've seen that smile." Rone rubbed his hands with force. "It's a thing of emptiness."

Charlotte nodded. "I'd almost forgotten you were in the guard. I'm not used to thinking of you like that. I only saw you in uniform that one time."

"It never fit right, and I looked bad in it. It's best you forget it entirely."

"No, I don't think so. That's one thing I don't want to forget. Anyway, my father scolded us, especially me, as wrestling is very-unladylike, but he got a letter from the Count a few days later. It was a marriage proposal, and apparently quite modest. I don't know why my father cared about political alliances in Veraland, but he agreed. I had to say goodbye to everything.

"We spent a few days in the castle in Vargana before we left, and that's when I overheard my uncle, the king, berating my father."

Charlotte frowned and looked at the wall as she spoke, "'The entire Catannel family is hideous and cruel. What a waste of a beautiful daughter. And for a political attachment you *don't need*,' my uncle said. I had been hiding in the larder, eating sugar, if you can believe that.

"I can, even though I have seen you eat wild rabbit," Rone said.

"Hunger makes everything sweet." Charlotte sighed. "My father was not receptive to my uncle. 'A good king would understand the need for his vassals to gather support for themselves, and in turn their ruler,' he said.

"'A good vassal would trust his king to secure peace for his charges,' my uncle said back.

'I will do what I think is best for my family, and my daughter, unless you think your providence extends to the very bedrooms of your subjects'

'You know my objections, Brut. It is your prerogative, but I would not choose to send my daughter across the sea.' I remember that so well – a feeling that it didn't have to be like it was.

"My father exploded, though. 'Your daughter would be a princess, and you would not even need a dowry to procure security for her. I do not have such luxuries. I am *lucky* to have what you consider an ugly and cruel family take her. Who would you prefer I let take her?'

"'I will take her. She can live here, in safety and luxury, and I will arrange a suitable marriage to a proper man of northern blood,' my uncle said. My heart leapt in hope, if only for a moment. It was as if in one moment I had dreams born, fulfilled, and then burned. I loved my uncle's house, you see, just like my mother did, and I could imagine meeting a handsome knight – chivalrous and bold – and loving him.

"'To hell with you, brother, and your insults. I will do what I wish with my own family,' was the last I heard. They didn't speak to each other again that I remember. My uncle caught me a day before I left and handed me a leather bag full of gold. He said it was a dowry for me or an early inheritance, and that I should keep it hidden and for myself. And that his castle would always be my home if I wanted it."

Rone nodded toward the baggage. "I wondered how you came by it."

"I had grand ideas of what I would do with it, at one point. I thought I could… hire an escape." Charlotte looked out the window, and a tear fell over one eyelid. "But why escape? That's what you want to know now, right?"

"I can be content with just the job," Rone said. "If that is what you want. My handler didn't give me details, and I'm used to it."

"It was a beautiful wedding, Rone. It was in a cathedral, with bright blue and green uniforms and a royal guard, officiated by the high cleric of Veraland. Catannel, his aids, his castle by the sea; they were all facades, like a stiff coat of paint over rotten wood. The real Catannel's heart matches his face.

"The first thing he did when we retreated to his apartments in the castle was slap me. I was shocked, but then he gripped my throat, squeezed, and smiled, and I understood. I fought him, and he did not leave uninjured, but as I found out in the weeks to come, that was exactly what he liked. He ripped my beautiful blue dress off without care to its quality. He held me down and forced his way into me despite my screams, laughing the whole time. Nobody came to help me. He raped me, Rone."

Charlotte hid her face in her hands and began to shudder. Rone hesitated a moment, then put his arm around her.

"You can stop."

Charlotte took a breath and continued from in her hands, "I was a virgin, but the pain… it was so bad, Rone. So much worse than anything other women had told me it would be. Afterward, he left me, bloody and crying on the bed, and locked the door from the outside." Charlotte raised her head, and though her face was wet with tears, she wore a stern, determined expression. "There was but one thing I was thankful for that night, and that was the fact that Sarthius did not think to go through my things. After he left, I was able to hide the money my uncle had given me.

"I found my mother the next day and told her. All she did was pat my back and say, "It always hurts the first time, you'll get over it." I did not know how to react. Part of me was confused, though I knew deep down what I had been subjected to could never be enjoyed. Sarthius found out about what I said to my mother and punished me. He proceeded to have my door kept locked when he or his servants could not directly observe me. Nobody in my family ever came to visit me."

"I think your uncle knew," Rone said. "Since it's him who hired me."

"It is?"

"I think so, anyway," Rone said. "I can't say for sure, as I was hired through an intermediary, which is standard, but I had and inkling once you told me he was your uncle. It's a lot of money. More than your little bag by a lot."

"Is that why you never took the money and ran?"

"No."

"Good, I need to hear you say that, Rone."

Rone touched her face lightly and turned her lips toward

his. He kissed her, very softly, then rubbed gently at the tear tracks on her cheeks. "If you don't want to go back to Hviterland, I'll take you wherever you want. I mean that. I have connections all through the Divine Strand. I don't need the money."

Charlotte shook her head. "No, I need to go home. And…" She sniffed softly, "he's evil. Not just to me. I couldn't satisfy him. He would often have his way with the servants or have girls from the city brought in. Somebody has to punish him. Vegard would. He will. He has the power."

"Maybe not just him," Rone said. "All men have a weakness. An arrow will kill a king as well as a beggar." Rone let his head hang. "My name is cursed for serving him, even for so short a time. I always knew something was wrong with him. You hear things – things I should have listened to but chose to disbelieve. A lot of the guards were in on it."

"They're just like him," Charlotte said.

"I hate him," Rone said. "I've spent my whole adult life being dispassionate, but I hate him. I'm so sorry he took so much from you."

Charlotte wrapped her arms around Rone's waist and pulled him closer to her on the bed. "Rone."

"I'm here," Rone said, wrapping his arms around her.

"I need you to be my hero, even if you're just in it for the money. Be a killer, but be my hero, too." They sat there for a few moments, then she said, "I'd forgotten that it can feel good to be touched."

"You still want me to go to the other room?"

"No. I want you close. I always want you close."

"I'll be close, then, but just close."

VII: Gold Courthouse

Rone woke up suddenly, snapping out of a dream in which he was lost in a forest where it was neither day nor night and everywhere he looked, he saw shades and ghosts. Some of the faces he recognized, but he lost all sense of who they belonged to as sleep left him. His pulse quickened as he realized that Charlotte was no longer beside him on the bed.

"Charlotte?" he said aloud, craning his neck to see if she was behind the privacy screen where the chamber pot sat. He could see nothing, so he pulled himself up. He still wore his clothes, though he had at least taken his boots off. After a quick look around the room, he realized he was truly alone. Breathing deeply to calm himself, he pulled on his boots, checked his pistol, and began to arm himself. When he went to strap on his sword belt, he noticed a small silver tray sitting on an occasional table.

Upon it sat an open razor, an stiff hairbrush, a small bowl of water, and a chunk of tallow soap. Rone noticed a small piece of paper and picked it up, finding a note written in an elegant hand that said:

You said you wanted to shave, so I asked the steward for a razor. I'm going to be brave today, but I expect to have you on hand. Meet me upstairs in the drawing-room when you are finished dressing. Wear what I bought you in Masala.

-C

Rone smiled, then set about to lighting a fire in the corner stove to heat the water.

*

"I haven't seen that face is quite a while," Charlotte said. She pulled off one of her lace-cuffed gloves and ran her palm over his cheeks. "I thought men were supposed to have rough skin." She straightened his doublet, then tightened the silk tie at the top.

"The beard helps protect it," Rone said. He looked Charlotte up and down and smiled. She was wearing a black dress, though she had pieces of delicate white lace lining the bust, hem, and sleeves. The top showed off just enough shoulder to turn a head, but not enough to be outside of formal traditions: her sleeves ended just below her elbow, leaving an expanse of skin between them and her gloves, and more lace covered where her breasts would be displayed in the top, though a crack of cleavage still peeked above. "Where did you get that outfit?"

"Mitha's wardrobe."

"She let you go through her wardrobe?"

"I told her serving maid I could."

"How deceptive of you," Rone said.

"I have a good teacher," she said. She took a sip of tea and smiled at the sky above the patio.

"So why did you want me to wear this again?" Rone said.

"Are you ready to help me be brave today?"

"You aren't brave now?"

"No," Charlotte said. "I'm terrified."

"That has nothing to do with courage." He picked up his cup of tea and took a sip. "Too much sugar," he said, though he kept drinking it. "After all you've been through getting here, you still think you're not brave?"

"I had you dragging me along. I need you to drag me again. I'm going to get Johnny out of prison,"

"How's that?" Rone said. "A prison break?"

"No, that's your area of expertise. I'm going to talk him out of prison."

"You think you can do that?"

"I'm very well-cultured, mister Stonefield, and I have a background in the art of rhetoric, as is fitting a woman of my stature."

"Alright," Rone said. "You have a plan? You hinted to as much last night."

"Yes. We're going to be Johnny's lawyers. I gathered from Mitha that this Gold Courthouse the nobles here use is very big on common law. I bet I can work out a way to get him off."

"And if you can't?"

"Then we're no worse off."

"Unless the courthouse figured out who we are, and hands us over to Vindrel."

"Would fugitives walk right into the prison?"

"No." Rone smiled at her. "Not unless they were stupid."

"Which is why they won't think we are Charlotte and Rone. They'll think we're… whoever we say we are."

Rone was silent for a moment. "I won't be much help with the talking, I think."

"Just stand there and look pretty." Again, Charlotte reached up and touched his face.

*

The Gold Courthouse was less a courthouse than a fortress, and though it was not made of gold like the old tales suggested, it earned its name as its primary concern was banking, not justice. It was like a small castle, with a tall outer wall and a fortified inner keep, but at the same time, it was open and airy, full of the bustle of people. Men and women of all social classes walked in and out freely, and the posted guards, all well-armed, were casual with their conversations.

Charlotte and Rone were paid little mind as they wandered in through the front gate.

There were a few tables in the courtyard dedicated to money changing, as the island, perched as it was in the sea, received coinage from all over Deideron. The interior of the keep was well-lit by skylights and tall steel-barred windows. Far across from the entrance stood a cashier's cage, and beyond it, steel doors and a treasure room. Hallways opened up to auxiliary rooms and stairs, some labeled with different services such as "Real Estate," "Personal Loans," "Hearings," and "Common Justice."

"Are you ready?" Charlotte asked, pausing beside the sign for "Internment, Bond Guarantee, Execution."

Rone nodded and opened the door. It led from the bright central hall of the Gold Courthouse down a narrow stair to the dungeon below ground level. They stepped into an office with barred windows where a small bearded clerk sat at a desk next to a guard armed with a halberd who was leaning by a massive, iron-bound door.

"Pardon me," Rone said. "I'm here to see a client."

The short clerk immediately stood up and smiled.

"Grant Smooty, at your service," he said. He looked to Charlotte and gave a shallow bow. He looked back to Rone. "Are you an attorney?"

"Not with the Gallow, but yes," Rone said.

"We both are, actually," Charlotte said. Rone coughed to himself.

"Of course," Grant said, bowing again, "I should have known from the dress; I just seldom see women in the profession here. Pardon my ignorance."

"Think nothing of it," Charlotte said, tilting her head in response. "I am Pelna Cans, and this is Morton Lindblum." She held her gloved hand toward Rone, who smiled and nodded.

"How can I help you?" Grant said.

"I believe you are holding an employee of ours," Charlotte said. "A mister Johnny."

"Oh yeah," Grant said. "Big, huge fellow, right? He wouldn't give us a last name."

"Hmn," Rone said. "I was hoping you'd have beaten it out of him." He laughed obnoxiously. Charlotte quickly joined him, and so did the clerk.

"The truth is I don't think the fellow has one. Orphan." Charlotte gave the clerk a false sad face. "Poor thing."

Grant rubbed the back of his neck. "Well, we've got him. Fugitive contract, right? Don't remember the fellow who was on about it."

"Vindrel?" Rone said.

"Yes, that sounds right," Grant said. "Do you know him?"

"He is known *to* us," Charlotte said. "Though I've never met him."

"Well, he wants to take him off-island," Grant said. "Which means we have to hold out for a proper judge. The hearing starts in…" He looked at a small wooden clock on the wall, "An hour or so, in case nobody told you." He shrugged. "They often don't tell anybody."

"I see," Charlotte said. "I assume you will release him to us in the meantime. Providing bail guarantee, of course."

"I'm sorry madam, I can't do that. Not for maritime crimes," Grant said.

"May we at least confer with our client?" Rone asked.

"Of course. Bert!" the clerk yelled.

The guard stepped forward with a grumble. "I'm right here, boss. No need to yell."

"Send these two down," Grant said. He looked at Charlotte. "We have another prisoner downstairs – nasty little man. Let me know if he gives you any trouble. I'll deal with him if he's uncouth."

Charlotte nodded, and they followed the guard down a sloping hallway.

"He likes to spit at people," Bert said sideways. "The little fellow, I mean. Try not to get too close." He knocked thrice on the door. "Visitors for that big chap."

The sounds of metal grinding against metal echoed in the narrow stairway, then the door swung inward. Rone glanced at the door frame and the wall surrounding it, noting the vault-like barring mechanism that sent four pieces of black steel into a reinforced channel in the wall. They stepped past another armed guard into the small dungeon, though that was perhaps too harsh a word for it. It was a tidy and bright jail, lit by small, square windows, double-barred and piping in light from a ground level that was above even the ceiling. A line of steel-barred cells went down one side of the room, each with a mattress, a chamber pot, and a wooden shelf. Only two of these were occupied. One was filled by a man who lay snoring in a small patch of sunlight on the hard floor. In the closer cell was Johnny, who was staring at the ceiling.

"There you are!" Rone shouted, "I hope you remember us, we're-"

"It's you!" Johnny said, bolting upright and half-stumbling to the cell door. "I didn't even recognize you without the-"

"Pelna Cans and Morton Lindblum," Charlotte said quickly and loudly. "We were attorneys for your ships majority holder in Golice. So glad you haven't forgotten us."

Johnny stared at them with a puzzled look for a moment, his hands hanging on the iron bars. "You work for… Tommy?"

Rone waved his hand in front of his face at Johnny's breath, which reeked of whiskey and barley beer, despite him being in prison for more than a day. "Yes," Rone said, eyes wide. "We argue at the court in Golice on behalf of... Tommy."

"Oh," Johnny said. He cracked his strange grin and winked very obviously. "Yeah, good 'ol Tom, and the lawyers, always with the lawyers... that fellow."

Charlotte's eyes were bulging as she subtly tried to wave her hands and get Johnny to stop talking. Rone looked over at the end of the row to see the guard sit down at a table and begin gnawing an apple. He opened up a nearby book and started reading.

"Tom?" Rone said quietly, leaning toward the bars. "You went with Tommy?"

"It's a name," Johnny said, shrugging. "It's familiar. Tommy is a kind name. A name you call a good friend. Like Johnny, eh?"

Rone and Charlotte looked at each other in confusion.

"Bah, the guard's an idiot anyway. He doesn't listen to anything down here."

"You're going before a judge in an hour, and we're going to try to deal for your freedom," Charlotte said. "Vindrel is here, and tried to arrest you, right?"

"You're talking like a lawyer already, lass," Johnny said. "And yeah, I guess you didn't manage to kill the bastard in Masala."

"I probably saved him, actually," Rone said. "I patched him up while you were dealing with shoving off after the mutiny."

"Why would you do a thing like that?" Johnny said.

Rone chewed his cheek silently.

"He knew him from before," Charlotte said.

"I couldn't leave him to die," Rone said. "Just leave it at that for now."

"Fine, but if this fellow sees me hanged, I'm gonna throttle you," Johnny said.

"How do you aim to do that?" Rone said.

"I have an army of assassins ready to throttle those that get me hanged, in the event of… my being hanged," Johnny said.

"Right," Charlotte said.

"You don't know," Johnny said. He burped.

Charlotte shook her head. "Are you still drunk?"

"Only a little," Johnny said.

"For a big man, you don't hold your liquor well," Rone said.

"You hadn't been seeing how much liquor I was holding yesterday. I'll be right as rain in half an hour."

"He said that three hours ago," the man in the other cell said loudly, sitting up. They recognized him as Mineo, the man who nearly lost his head in the public square.

"Bah, you're just jealous," Johnny said.

"I am," Mineo said. "You know how hard it is to get a sniff in this pit? Now shut up! Some of us are trying to piddle away the hours of our day over here." His head popped up, and he raised an eyebrow to Charlotte. She tried not to return the glance and focus on Johnny. "Hey, pretty," he said.

"Pardon me," Charlotte said, then looked at Johnny again.

"How about you let me see what you've got behind all that black lace? You know I'm doomed to die."

"I should say so," Rone said. Charlotte put her hand on his chest firmly.

"C'mon, lass," Mineo said. "How about just one tit? I promise to think about it when the lights are out. What do you say, one sweet pink nipple for a dying man's pleasure?"

"Just ignore him," Johnny said. "Poor sod will be dead soon anyway."

Charlotte and Rone turned back to Johnny.

"Do you know anything about how the courts work here?"

she said.

"Not really," Johnny said. "I think they just enforce contracts, near as I can tell. Common law stuff. You have to hire the court to try a criminal here."

"The clerk outside said something about arbitration and restitution," Charlotte said.

Johnny shrugged.

"Maybe we can rummage through some rule books or something upstairs," Charlotte said. He looked at Johnny and said, "Otherwise, I'll have to get creative. We'll see you in an hour. Wish us luck."

"I'm *cursing* my luck right now mister, uh, Lindgren," Johnny said as the turned to walk away.

"Lindblum!" Rone whispered back as he and Charlotte walked toward the exit. Without taking his eyes off his book, the Jailor stood up and began turning a wheel on the back of the door. Rone took one last quick look around, taking in the details and features of the underground jail before following a guard out of the door.

*

"This is the law library?" Charlotte asked, pulling out wooden bins of paper from the shelves, and pawing through them quickly. "There's nothing here but contracts."

"That's what the law is," the old bald clerk said from nearby. He was busy stamping forms with a square hunk of carved wood. He turned around to regard Charlotte for a moment. "Well, other than theft, or rape, or murder, but nobody needs to write any of that down."

"This is hopeless," Charlotte said. She eyed the clock sitting on the clerk's desk. The minute hand seemed to have jumped several spaces ahead.

"Maybe there's something I can help you with," the clerk said.

"We have a friend – a client," Rone said, "that was arrested and jailed. He has a hearing with a judge at the top of the hour."

"Well, the judge will sort it out," the old man said, writing something on a card and putting it to the side of his desk. "Of course, if you feel the need to argue, you can pull the correct contract here."

"Contract?" Charlotte said. "For an arrest?"

The old man looked at her. "Yes… well, where was he arrested?"

"In a pub, I believe," Rone said.

"Belonging to whom?" The old smiled slightly.

"I believe it was called… Reggets," Charlotte said. The old man cleared his throat. She looked down to see an open palm. She quickly pulled a silver coin from her purse and put it in his hand. He smiled as he tucked it into his jacket pocket, then stood up and walked across the crowded room.

He opened up a cabinet revealing long rows of stiff paper and began pawing through them and mumbling to himself. "Regget Harrity, Regget Harritty… ah, here he is." He pulled up a small card containing columns of scribbled words and neatly stamped dates. "Two-'C' looks to be the correct spot. He put the card down and walked to one of the bins. After a moment of rummaging, he produced a short set of printed words with a few signatures attached. He handed it to Charlotte. "This is his contract with the courthouse for arrest and security services."

Charlotte turned it over in her hand. "This is it?"

"Yes," the old man said, putting the card back in the large wooden cabinet and walking back toward his desk. "Anything the courthouse is either allowed or obligated to do is in that contract." He smiled. "Good luck, and be sure to bring that back before you go."

The door to the closet-like room opened, and Charlotte and Rone turned to see Teal Starnly, wearing a crisp grey jacket with black long pants enter, a leather satchel under his arm. "Ah, there you two are," he said. "Johnny's hearing will be in a few minutes."

"What are you doing here?" Charlotte said.

Starnly walked up and pulled the contract from her hands and glanced at it. "Thank you." He looked back at them and said, "I'm here to argue Johnny's case for you."

"You are?" Charlotte said.

He smiled. "I'm an attorney, after all. Even if the Gallow doesn't have much use for us, I prefer to flex the argument muscles from time to time." He motioned them to follow him out of the room. "I was hoping you could persuade your friend to agree to our contract. He seemed a little untrusting of me."

"I can't blame him. I don't particularly trust you, after all."

"Mister Stonefield," Starnly said, putting his hand to his chest, "I'm offended."

"Actually, it's mister Lindblum now," Rone said.

"And I'm Miss Cans," Charlotte said.

Teal chuckled. "I presume you are pretending to be lawyers?"

"Yes," Charlotte said. "In the employ of one Tom of Golice, majority shareholder of the Parkitees."

"What's his last name?" Sean said.

"I... didn't get one, I think," Charlotte said.

"Well, make one up," Starnly said as he set off again, crossing the busy central room. "You appear to be good at it. Now, my fellow solicitors, let's get to the courtroom, and please," he looked back at Charlotte, "*Do* use some of that charm on the judge." He glanced at her breasts, hidden slightly with lace, then winked at her.

"Wait," Rone said. Starnly paused and raised his eyebrows.

"Do you think Vindrel could be in there?"

"Is that the fellow that caught your captain?" Sean said.

"Yes," Rone said.

"Then most certainly," Sean said. "He'll either be wanting restitution or to get ahold of your friend. Don't worry, we won't allow it."

"We'd best not go in, then," Rone said, "as long as we have you to speak for Johnny. He could recognize us."

"He won't recognize me," Charlotte said. "He's never seen me, remember? Only certain people from Cataling ever got to look at me."

"That's right, but he *will* recognize me." Rone paused and thought for a moment. "I'll catch you afterward, alright?"

"Very good," Starnly said.

VIII: Games of Chance

The inside of the courtroom was very different from those that Charlotte had experienced in her younger days. Rather than a wide hall well-lit with large windows, centered around a platform that made the judge tower over criminals and litigants alike, the courtroom at the Gold Courthouse was a small stone chamber, more like a receiving room or an office than a theater of justice. A few wooden chairs were arrayed before small desks that faced a massive walnut table heaped with papers. A few novel chandeliers that scattered light from the skylights were also present, bathing the room in a constant yet slightly too-dim glow.

Charlotte followed Teal Starnly in through the door and to a set of desks on the left side of the small room. She noticed a tall and lean man, presumably Regget, the owner of the bar, sitting at a desk in the center of the arc. He smiled at her as she walked past him. She glanced over him to a large man clad in blue and green, with a black beard and hazy yellow-green eyes, who leaned against a chair, letting his left arm, which was in a sling, rest upon the desk before him. Her heart quickened a bit as she thought twice about whether the man would recognize her. She had not explored much of Catannel's castle in Cataling, being more or less a captive during her two years there, and did not know whether the count had procured any of the many paintings that existed of her from her youth. She considered for the first time that Vindrel could indeed have seen her before, in a painting hung far outside her prison-like bedroom.

"I can't believe the pirate has lawyers," Vindrel said with a growl to a middle-aged man beside him in a similar uniform.

He glanced at Charlotte, and she shuttered inwardly. She took a shallow breath and calmed herself, feeling more confident that he didn't at least immediately recognize her. *Besides,* she thought, *He's not expecting me to just walk in here.* She smiled at him and he looked away.

"Pirates are the only men I can think of who need them," said the man sitting beside Vindrel. His accent was posh, almost exaggerated.

"Be sure to tell that to the judge," Starnly said with a smile. The posh man laughed.

"I wonder whose mistress this one is," Vindrel said, nodding toward Charlotte.

"Certainly I'll never be yours," Charlotte said, keeping hold of her voice but unable to resist the bait of the insult, "Though with a face like that I imagine you could bed any bitch in the kennel."

"I'll show you how I bed a bitch," Vindrel said, standing. "Do you know who you're talking to, woman?"

Starnly put his hand lightly on Charlotte's shoulder as if to restrain her. She stared back and Vindrel and said, her voice finally quavering, "I'm talking to a… petty little man, working for another petty little man." She took a quick, shallow breath, clenching her fists, and trying to keep her voice even. "Who King Borlond would refuse to hire as a jailor in the dirtiest dungeon holding the worst men in Golice."

Vindrel moved his right arm as if reaching for a pistol under his sling, but straightened his face and stood still as an old wooden door on the other side of the room opened up and an older man entered, dressed in a black jacket and long pants, all trimmed with gold. He had deep, dark brown skin and curly black hair, but his eyes were a pale green, and his hair had faded from black to a slate grey on the temples.

"Afternoon, gents," the man said as he crossed to the large table facing them. He put some papers down, looked up, and, noticing Charlotte, said, "And Lady." Among the documents was a small triangular nameplate, which he set at the front of the table. Upon a brass plate could be read in etching, "Charles Delving."

"Your honor," she said with a nod.

He looked back at her with a wide smile. "You must be from the mainland. We do things a bit differently here. *You* can just call me Charles, none of the 'your honor' business."

"Of course," Charlotte said, nodding again. Starnly tugged on her glove as she sat down, prompting her to follow him into the wooden chair beside his.

"Good to see you again, Teal," the judge said.

"You too, Chuck," Starnly said with a smile. "Good to see the law is treating you well."

"She treats me fairly," Chuck said with a wink. "When are you going to take the board up on that offer? Get on the other side of the bench for a change."

"Maybe during retirement," Starnly said. "Until then, I'm having far too much fun in the shipping business."

"Try not to get too rich," the judge said. "Or you'll be able to buy a house too far up the hill. You'll love the walk down, but the walk back will kill you, especially when you get to be my age." The old man pulled a set of half-glasses from his pocket and put them on, reading silently from one of the papers in his stack. "Well, let's get down to business. You two can sit any time you like," he said, looking at Vindrel and the other officer. The two men in uniform exchanged a glance and then seated themselves.

The door through which the judge had entered swung

open again, and two guards came in with Johnny between them. He was in loose-fitting chains: two sets of irons locked together to accommodate his immense height and girth. One of the guards, holding an oversized brass-locked blunderbuss, motioned for Johnny to sit in a nearby chair. Johnny frowned but complied.

"Let's go through it for the record," the judge said, dipping a pen into an inkwell.

"May I have a brief consultation with my client?" Starnly said. "He still needs to sign the retainer." Starnly looked over at Charlotte and nodded slightly.

"That's right," Charlotte said, looking at Johnny. "We're prepared to cover local expenses, captain."

"Oh, of course," the judge said. "We don't want to be working for free, eh?"

"I'm a rich man," Starnly said, crossing the room to Johnny with a thick contract in his hands. "I mostly do it for fun, anyway."

Johnny stared at Charlotte for a moment after Starnly handed him the papers and a freshly dipped pen. He shrugged and signed, then initialed the other pages. Starnly smiled at Johnny and brought the contract back to his own desk, flapping the last page to dry the ink.

"Alright, where were we?" the Judge said, freshening his pen. "Oh yes... Parties present?" He pointed to Charlotte, then to each man to her right in turn.

"Pelna Cans," Charlotte said. "Representation from the court of Golice. Arguing for Johnny." The judge scrawled quickly on a paper in front of himself.

"Teal Starnly," Sean said beside her. "Representing Ashroad Shipping Incorporated, arguing for the same."

"Let's not forget representation for our dear Gallow," Charles said, scribbling. He pointed to the man in the center.

"Regget Harity," he said. "Representing myself and arguing for myself, and my property, Regget's Pub."

The officer Vindrel had brought with him cleared his throat when the judge pointed at him. "Admiral-Lord Donovan Dunneal, supreme commander of the combined fleet of the Veraland, the Green Isle, subject to his majesty King Sarthius Catannel of Cataling."

The judge looked up with a raised eyebrow. "New king is news to me." The admiral cleared his throat again, which prompted a contemptuous look from the judge. "And... who exactly are you arguing for, mister Dunneal?"

Donavan stood mute for a moment. "For justice."

"Then you'd best find a box and a street corner, admiral," the judge said. "We don't do justice here; we interpret contracts and the law." Teal chuckled, and the judge winked at him.

"Then we are arguing for the Isle," Donovan said.

"Very well," the judge said. He pointed at Vindrel.

"Vindrel Stonefield," he said. Charlotte's heart raced for a minute as she heard the name. "Chief inquisitor and minister of security to his majesty King Sarthius Catannel of Veraland. Arguing for myself, my king, and against Johnny."

The judge scribbled again and pointed to Johnny.

"Johnny. Um. Arguing for myself?"

"Johnny what?" the judge said.

"Just Johnny."

The judge looked over at Charlotte, who said, "He lacks a family name that we know of."

"Very well, Just Johnny it is," the judge said. He held up a paper slightly and read a few lines to himself. "I am Charles Delving-" The admiral cleared his throat, and the judge looked up, cocking his head. "Do you have something to say before proceedings, mister Dunneal?"

The admiral cleared his throat again. "Nothing, just a familiar name."

"He must be thinking of Seamus Delving," Charlotte said.

The judge looked over at her with a smile. "Ah, Seamus," the judge said before looking back at Donovan. "He's my little brother." The admiral cleared his throat again, almost coughing. "Yes?"

"He's…" The admiral raised his eyebrows, his face slack with shock. "Well, he's wanted for piracy."

"In Veraland, no doubt," the judge said, "but this is not the Green Isle and were you to say something like that in Datalia, I think you might be laughed out of the room. Seamus is a war hero, even if he is a privateer. And a good brother to boot." The judge chuckled, looking at his paper again, mumbling something from which only the word "manners" Charlotte could make out. He looked at Regget. "So, we had a little altercation in your pub, in which this large fellow," he pointed at Johnny, "was getting the better of this fellow." He pointed at Vindrel.

"That's right, mister Delving," Regget said. "The guard has already been paid in cash. I have a receipt if you need it. Asking for the right to recover my loss."

"Granted," the judge said. He looked at Johnny. "Any contest?"

Johnny looked back up and shrugged. "I was pummeling him if that's what you mean."

"Did you do that to his arm?" the judge asked.

"That? No, that wasn't me," Johnny said.

"Very well," the judge said. "Not contested, which surprises me. How much do you want in recompense?" He looked at Vindrel.

"Recompense?" Vindrel said. "He's a criminal!"

The judge sighed and looked at Regget, who said,

"Standard fare, mister Delving. I'd say 20 argents ought to do it."

"Objections?" the judge said to Vindrel.

The admiral cleared his throat again. "Charles-"

"That's mister Delving to you," the judge said.

"But you said to call you Charles," Donovan said.

"I said *she* could call me Charles," the judge said, nodding toward Charlotte. "You can call me Mister Delving." He looked back at Charlotte. "I tell you, people from the Isle never have any manners."

"I have learned this," Charlotte said.

The admiral cleared his throat again.

"You really ought to go see a doctor about that cough, admiral," the judge said.

"We are prepared to pay mister Harity's suggested restitution, given his experience in such matters," Starnly said, "As well as reimburse him for the court costs."

"Seems pretty straightforward," the judge said.

"Mister Delving," Donovan said, his voice rising to a near shriek. "We came here expecting you to turn over to us a wanted pirate; this isn't about his assault of the inquisitor at all. He murdered soldiers of the Isle in cold blood not a fortnight ago!"

"Mister Delving," Starnly said calmly, holding up the paper Rone and Charlotte had been given by the clerk earlier, "We have a copy of the contract between the courthouse and Regget Harity. It has the standard exceptions in place for accusations of piracy." Sean stood up and pushed the paper in front of the judge. "You'll notice that in criminal or bounty pursuits, the court is to disregard accusations of piracy if the subject in question was acting within the private prize contracts of his port of call, in this case, Golice."

"I can testify to that end," Charlotte said. "Johnny has a

contract with his Majesty, King Borlond Mothanan of Golice, and we assert that his actions have been within the scope of that contract." While she spoke, a door in the back opened and swung shut. Charlotte looked over for a moment and saw the familiar face of Farthow, now wearing a green jacket and maroon pants. He approached Vindrel, and, making eye contact with Charlotte, winked.

"We also assert," Starnly said, filling in the silence, "That any actions that may or may not have taken place between parties were at sea and therefore subject to private contract and maritime law."

"This is nonsense," Vindrel said, pushing himself up. "This man murdered soldiers of the Isle and his own first mate!" Farthow passed a note to Vindrel as he spoke. He looked down at it, frowning.

"What happens at sea is not the concern of the courthouse," the judge said. "Our laws end there. You can try to blast him out of the water once he leaves, but this is a free port, and I can't turn a man over on mere accusation of piracy." He cocked his head as Vindrel pushed his way past the admiral and Farthow.

"Excuse me, sir," Vindrel said. "Pressing business of the crown." He walked out the door briskly.

The admiral cleared his throat. "The actions we are talking about did not happen at sea, mister Delving, they happened on the docks at Masala."

The judge scratched his chin a moment and looked at Johnny, who shrugged.

"Mister Delving," Starnly said. "I must argue a few things. First, who was witness to this?"

"Vindrel was there himself, and injured," the admiral said.

"It's a pity he just left. We could have worked out an agreement to that right now," the judge said.

"We intend to hang the pirate," Donavan said.

"Second," Starnly said, "Mister Dunneal and Mister Stonefield are representatives of the County of Cataling, not Masala, which is under the rule of Drath Harec. Under standard rules of the court, accusations must come from those authorized to make them."

"I speak for the King of Veraland," Donavan said. "He has authority over all ports on the Green Isle.

"Charles," Charlotte said, "I'm afraid mister Donavan is not being truthful. Sarthius Catannel has not yet ascended to the throne, and will not until he can produce a wife."

"What do you mean by 'produce a wife'?" said the judge.

"This man is a party in the kidnapping of the queen!" the admiral said, pointing at Johnny.

"That's a laugh," Johnny said with a smile. "Me stealing off with the queen." He looked at the judge. "I mean, look at me, sir. Do I look like I could pull that off?"

"That's two lies, mister Dunneal," the judge said. "I'm going to have to give summary judgment for Regget and judge according to Teal's suggestions, agreeing with the argument of lack of authority."

"You would risk everyone on your island for a fat pirate?" the admiral said, leaning over the desk. "I'll have you know-"

The judge laughed. "You think I don't know about that antique fleet of yours sitting outside the harbor? I think if you put your guns to use, you'd get quite more than you bargained for in a fight with Tyrant's Gallow. We protect our own here, and there are many men here just as competent as my brother. Now, unless you have some other means of establishing authority, I'm going to send you off twenty argents heavier and mister Just Johnny free."

"I'm sure," the admiral said, breathing deeply, "that mister Bitterwheat will speak with authority for count Harec." He turned his hand as if to gesture at Farthow, only to see an empty seat right behind him. Donavan turned to see a greet coat disappearing out the door. "Farthow, get back here!" he shrieked.

The green jacket froze, then Farthow turned back into the little courtroom. "I have other business to attend to, Donny," he said, a look of annoyance on his face.

"You will address me as admiral Dunneal," he said, his voice cracking.

"I will address you as such when you are named such," Farthow replied as he strode up to the side of Donavan. "Till then, you are Donny."

"What do you say, mister… Bitterwheat?" the judge said. "Is this man a criminal?"

Fathow looked at Donavan uncomfortably for a moment. "He did have a scuffle with the Cataling guard while at dock in Masala."

"But not with the Masala guard," Charlotte said.

"No, not with the Masala guard," Farthow said.

"Is it a crime to do such?" the judge said.

"The count…" Farthow's face drooped as he glanced at Charlotte, "did allow the Cataling guard to pursue some men on the docks."

"They set up a mutiny on my ship!" Johnny said, standing up quickly. The guard standing near at hand put his hand on the large man's shoulder as if to push him down, but Johnny didn't give.

"The guard wants you to sit down, captain," Charlotte said.

Johnny looked about. "Oh," he said and flopped back into his chair.

"Well, there appears to be more to it than a little scuffle in your pub," Charles said, looking at Regget. "Life is interesting, no?"

Regget nodded, wide-eyed.

"Mister Delving," Starnly said. "I would just like to remind the court of its own policy, also stated in the contract, that transfers from in-house to out-of-country of a criminal nature can only be approved by a three-judge panel."

"Of course," the judge said. "May I keep this contract copy until tomorrow?" he held up the piece of paper Charlotte had found.

"You may file it again with the clerks at your leisure," Starnly said.

"Very well," the judge said. "I'll gather up the other angry old men, and we'll have a hearing tomorrow with the three of us. Let's say ten in the morning." He turned to one of the guards. "By the way, Gunny, you can unchain the ship. It's a criminal matter now, apparently, and we've already agreed to compensation, so no need to keep things impounded."

"Yes sir, I'll have it done within the hour," the bailiff said.

"Mister Delving!" Donavan said as the judge stood up. "It's a pirate ship. You cannot be serious!"

"You can't put a criminal claim upon property. Until ten tomorrow, sirs and madam," Charles said, taking his glasses back off. He looked back at Charlotte with a smile, "Certainly not soon enough. Keep in mind you already agreed to twenty argents if I side with you."

"I will, Charles," Charlotte said.

The judge nodded and stepped out of the room.

"We did our best," Charlotte said to Johnny as he was pulled up and led toward the door in the back.

"Tell Danny's mum I went out smiling," he said back over his shoulder.

Starnly gave Charlotte a puzzled look. She shrugged. Donavan glared at her for a protracted moment and then stomped out of the room, the hard heels of his boots clicking loudly in the small chamber.

As the door swung behind him, Farthow leaned over and said quietly. "Sorry, I couldn't lie right in front of him."

"It's alright," Charlotte said. "What did you hand to Vindrel?"

"A note from Rone," Farthow said. "Telling Vindrel to meet him in a bar. He said he'd find you when he's done."

Charlotte felt a sudden fear. "What is he planning on doing?"

"Who knows with him?" Farthow said.

"We should wait for him at Seamus's house. He'll be having tea soon."

"Good idea. I'll send him your way."

Charlotte took a deep breath, watched the door out of which Johnny had vanished for a few moments, then followed Teal and Farthow out of the room.

*

"Somehow I knew your captain would lead you to this shit-hole of an island," Vindrel said as he approached Rone's table at the back of the second floor of the pub. A large window was open to the breeze, and the distant edge of the Gold Courthouse was visible. The afternoon sun cast a harsh beam across the floor to their right, and dust and ash danced visibly as Vindrel sat down at the little table.

"Did you just guess that, or did you see the same thing we saw on our way in?" Rone took a sip of his beer. He left his back to the corner of the upper floor and frequently glanced at the well-dressed men to each side of himself.

"It just seemed like a good destination for a bad pirate and a worse spy."

"You're not a good liar," Rone said.

"You're right. I'm nothing like you."

Rone looked away casually, but not so far that Vindrel was out of his periphery. "Don't you think it's unwise of your count to send his fleet away from his homeland and unwise for you to send it *here*, having seen Nantien for yourself?" Rone smiled as a young woman appeared from the spiral stair carrying a cluster of glass mugs in each hand. She smiled back at him as she began to place beers in front of other customers.

"You know nothing of the world of nobility, Rone."

"I know more than you would think, Vinny," Rone said.

"Just like an assassin to think himself a lord. You're a tool, nothing more." Vindrel quietly regarded the waitress as she put a mug of dark ale in front of him. "But whose tool, eh?"

"I took the liberty," Rone said with a smile. "It's not Black Cliff, but I think it will suit you."

Vindrel took a long drink, his eyes fixed on Rone. "My tastes have changed."

"So have mine." Rone held up his glass. "Pale ale. Bitter is all I can stand now."

"Unsurprising."

"Change… I guess that's life, eh?"

Vindrel wiped his mouth, still staring into Rone's eyes. "You're trying to tell me you've changed?"

"It's different this time, Vinny."

"How? Enough money to finally retire?" Rone shrugged at him. "That's a laugh." Vindrel looked away for a moment with a forced smile. "It's never enough money for men like you."

"In a way, you're right." Rone reached into his jacket pocket, his eyebrows high in an expression of peace, and withdrew an old deck of cards. He placed them in the center of the table.

"What's this?" Vindrel said.

"I said I'd play you for what I have the next time I saw you."

Vindrel took another long drink, then picked up the deck. He glanced down at it, then back at Rone, as if he feared the man would disappear if he but looked away. He flipped the deck over and looked through the cards. "There are no dragons," he said.

"I used them all up cheating," Rone said. "But it makes the odds easier."

Vindrel shuffled. The old cards were notched and misshapen, not snapping back to shape after the shuffle. "What do you have to play with?"

"I'm afraid I'm a little short on funds," Rone said. "Poker is never fun with a poor man."

"What will you wager instead?"

"My life," Rone said. Vindrel paused to look at him. "The things that go with it. We can do whatever game you like; it doesn't matter to me. If you win, I'll give myself up. You can walk me right on to your ship and haul me away."

"I aim to have that prize anyway," Vindrel said. "What's to stop me from just killing you right here?"

Rone held his palms forward. "If you have it in you. You didn't all those years ago, and I don't think you have it in you now."

"Change, right?"

Rone nodded. "If I win, you turn away. You take your ships, and you leave. Go back and defend our home against the Dreasenith Empire."

"The Empire is nothing," Vindrel said.

"Will you take the wager, or not?" Rone said.

"You aren't what I want," Vindrel said. "I need the girl."

Rone chuckled. "You really don't. You can say she's dead. I'm sure it makes no difference to Catannel. Her personhood is meaningless beyond the fact that he married her. He can marry someone else."

"You said yourself I'm a bad liar," Vindrel put the cards on the table. "But, like *I* said, you don't understand nobility. She matters, or do you think Catannel would bother otherwise?"

Rone raised an eyebrow at the revelation.

"You put the girl up, and you've got a game."

"I can't do that, Vinny."

"And why is that?" Vindrel said. "Did she cut you loose already?"

"I'm the wager. Me." Rone reached out and cut the deck.

"I'll leave you room to raise that wager." Vindrel picked it back up and began dealing. "I assume you will find Denarial's high-game acceptable?" Two cards were now face down in front of Rone and Vindrel. He put two more at the center of the table, then flipped two more face-up in front of each of them.

The ten of mountains and the queen of plains sat in front of Vindrel. Rone had the knight of plains and the two of forests.

"Why this game? I already listed the stakes."

"I said I'd give you room to raise your wager." Vindrel pulled the edge of his cards off the table and looked at them. He had two queens: mountains and forests

"Yes but can you raise yours?" Rone picked up his cards and looked at them. He smiled.

"Perhaps I won't just yet," Vindrel said. "We'll let the opening hand be your suggestion, and then we can go up from there. Perhaps I will offer that you give me the girl and let you go, eh?"

Rone laughed and turned his cards over, pushing them close to the center of the table. "You can run this game however you like, Vinny." There sat the two of mountains and the eight of rivers.

Vindrel looked at Rone's hand and tried to stuff a smile.

"I'll let you fold now if you like. You can just follow me back to the ship right now." Rone stared back at him, calmly. Vindrel picked up the deck and put another card face down, then added one to the center: the two of plains. "No dragons in the roost today, Rone. You'll have to win a full set. I'll raise you the girl, and I'll promise to let you escape."

"It's your game to do with as you like," Rone said with a smile. "You can see my cards."

Vindrel chuckled. "I'm trying to help you, Rone."

"If you want to help me, then fold and leave," Rone said.

"All I've done is try to help you," Vindrel said, his voice growing in volume and drawing the attention of a few nearby patrons. "Since we were boys, I've shown you nothing but mercy. I've tried to get you good, honest, work and you spit in my face."

"You and I have different ideas of honest work," Rone said. He nodded toward the table. "Go on, play. It's your game."

"You're just the same spoiled child you always were," Vindrel said. "You haven't changed." He put one more card face down and flipped the last one in the middle. It was the two of rivers. His eyes widened. His gaze went up to Rone's, who looked back calmly.

"I guess you can still fold," Rone said.

"How…" Vindrel frowned. He picked up the deck and looked through it again. Nothing was missing or added, other than the fifth suite of dragons that normally trumped the others. "How did you…"

"I've never had it in me to kill you before, Vinny," Rone said, his eyes blazing with sudden intensity, "even when you practically begged me to do it. The truth is, I don't want to kill you now, but by the will of the dreamer, I will. It's worth it to me this time. If you force me too, I will end you. You are walking in *my* dream. It may be your game, but I control the cards." Rone downed the rest of his pale ale and stood up. He swept the cards into a pile and stuffed them into his jacket pocket.

Vindrel grabbed his arm. "You can't just walk away from this."

"I did, I can, and I will," Rone said. "We'll find out tomorrow which of us is the real liar." He shook Vindrel's grip from his arm and disappeared down the spiral staircase.

After a moment of shock, Vindrel broke his paralysis and rushed down after him, dashing toward the front double doors of the inn. When he appeared in the street, all he could see were the ambling masses of people moving among the merchants in the market. He looked around frantically, searching around the building, but Rone was gone.

"Hey, Greenman!" Vindrel turned to see the one-eyed grey-headed barkeeper. He had a pistol in one hand, hanging down. "You can't just leave without paying."

"Bastard," Vindrel said to himself, searching his pockets for coins.

IX: The Goods

Charlotte had a hard time focusing, though everyone else sitting at the ornate steel table seemed relaxed and amiable. Starnly had brought her to the estate of the famous Seamus Delving. Mitha had coincidentally (or not; Charlotte had not yet decided on how-well informed the woman truly was) been at the house visiting with him.

The conversation was interesting, and Seamus's many stories of adventures both humorous and exhilarating should have cheered Charlotte. Instead, she seemed only to be able to focus on the afternoon sun finding its way through the trellis above them, irritating her eyes. She let out a sigh of relief when Rone finally appeared, the gruff guard closing the gate behind him with a clang.

"Come now," Mitha said, smiling at her, "Seamus's stories are not *that* boring."

"Let the lass have her sighs," Seamus said.

Charlotte bowed to Mitha, Starnly, and Seamus Delving, as she stood up from the little table and left them to finish their tea.

"So, like I was saying," Seamus went on, "she said she was the queen. I took her for a liar, but as it would turn out, I was just making assumptions, as she never said just who or what she was queen of…"

Seamus's voice faded as Charlotte ran forward to Rone, wrapping her arms around him in a tight hug.

"I was only gone a few minutes," Rone said with a chuckle.

"What were you doing with him? He's the enemy."

"Just a friendly conversation," he said, "and a wager."

"Wager?"

"I bet my life on a hand of cards, that he would leave and go home," Rone said. "I won."

She twisted her fingers into the fabric of his jacket. "That was stupid."

"I'm sorry." He held her hands, which were gripping his doublet iron-tight. "But I don't think he would have killed me or hauled me off, even if he won the wager."

"You don't know that," Charlotte said, shaking him with her knotted hands.

"I do."

"How?"

"He's my brother, Charlotte."

She looked up into his eyes, feeling her vision tremble and blur, then looked down at the ground.

"He's my brother. We grew up together in the dry highlands. He offered me a job in the Cataling guard when I returned to Veraland, knowing what I did… as a profession, before. He's had other chances to kill me…" Rone sighed. "He wouldn't have had it in him."

Tears were collecting in her eyes. "Don't do that again," she said. "You put us at risk."

"I promise, I didn't put you at risk. I bet my own life, not yours."

"I said you put *us* at risk," Charlotte said, pulling back to look at him. "Us. That's you and me. I need you, Rone."

Rone breathed deeply, then forced out a small laugh. "Have a little faith." He pushed his thumbs into her fists, opening them a little. "I rather like this silly jacket. It was given to me by someone I care about, so try not to destroy it."

Charlotte was crying, but she laughed anyway, collapsing as she leaned against him. He hugged her again, then said,

"You were very brave today. I take it your gamble didn't work, as I don't see our captain."

"No, it didn't," Charlotte said.

"It'll be alright." He led her back toward the small table, where a servant was pouring an extra cup of tea.

"I don't think It's likely my brother will sell your friend out," Seamus said, making eye contact with Rone, then Charlotte. "We've had fleets knock on our door before. Salty privateers like myself tend to find remarkable ways to work together when pressed to it. The city is in no danger, and my brother will understand that."

"No doubt, especially if the city is filled with men like you," Rone said.

"I trust by that you mean proper gentlemen," Seamus said and winked.

"I suppose one could be a gentlemen *and* warrior." He sat down with Charlotte and took a sip of the tea. It was hot and had a pale color and flavor like the tea Mitha had served the day before. Rone looked away, watching one of the fruit trees in Seamus's courtyard wave in the afternoon breeze. "I made a play with Vindrel. If he acts like his old self, he'll have a hard time declining honor and showing up to the hearing tomorrow."

"You sound doubtful," Farthow said.

Rone looked at him. "I am. It's another gamble, and I prefer not to leave things to chance."

"Yet you played a game of chance with him," Charlotte said.

"You're right, of course. I keep things stacked in my favor, but there are always risks."

"The chance is part of what makes the play worthwhile," Mitha said. "Nothing ventured, nothing gained."

"Spoken true," Seamus said. He looked at Rone and folded

his hands, smirking. "Mitha and I have selected a good crew for you. Competent sailors that men like *us* can trust."

Rone looked over at Starnly and detected a slight smile.

*

The hour of tea had ended spontaneously, with Mitha and then Seamus excusing themselves for other business. Being left alone at the table with a strange servant standing near at hand with tea kettle had felt strange, so after a minute or so, Charlotte and Rone excused themselves, telling the servant to be sure to thank Seamus for his hospitality. Farthow met them just as they were leaving through the courtyard gate.

"You got your shopping list?" Rone said to Farthow. He tapped his temple.

"Shopping, eh?" Charlotte said with a smile. "Looking for another outfit?"

"That's not quite what I had in mind," Rone said.

"Then what?" Charlotte said. They began to walk back downhill, away from the towering estates of high-town and toward the central square, the road twisting, but slowly widening. When they caught sight of the square, the central stage was occupied again, this time by what looked like a slave auction.

"The Gallow is a fine place to purchase items of less than legal status." Rone cracked a wry smile at Charlotte.

Charlotte cocked her head. "You want to get into the slave business?"

"Dreamer, no," Rone said. "I'm a man of principle. Just the smuggling business, thank you."

"I have a feeling you are already traveling with smugglers," Farthow said.

"Johnny? Trafficking? Perish the thought," Charlotte said, waving her hand at Farthow.

Rone stopped and looked down the street toward the

bustling central square below. "Think we could slip back by the jail?" Rone said.

"I suppose," Farthow said. "Need to have another look?"

Rone smiled at Farthow. "Oh, I just want a word with the captain. You know, I figured I'd better clear things up with him before I fill his hull with tar."

Fathow smiled but shook his head. "Alright, they didn't catch onto you the first time."

"The Courthouse isn't looking for us," Rone said. "I get the impression they don't really care about what Vindrel wants, in an active way."

"You know, Johnny could probably give us some snappy advice on just what will sell well in Golice," Farthow said.

"You're serious, aren't you?" Charlotte said, looking up at Rone with a frown. "We don't need to smuggle. I have plenty of coin."

Rone looked ahead. "We already promised Johnny a big payout in Golice-"

"*If* he ever goes free," Charlotte said.

Rone nodded. "Yes, *if*." Charlotte watched Rone's face carefully, not liking the inward gaze he had, which refused to meet her own. "We will still need plenty of money to get you to Hviterland after we reach Golice, but there's more to it."

"What then?" Charlotte said.

Rone took a breath and stopped in the street. "There are entrenched systems devoted to avoiding detection. They are present in every city and every region. Probably even here in Tyrant's Gallow. They're involved in illicit trade, and I want to make use of the people in those systems. These are people who know how to get in and out of places discreetly. While I'm worried about getting into and out of Golice, I'm just as worried about Vargana."

"Why the concern? That's home. My uncle is the king,"

Charlotte said.

"The Draesenith Empire. War is brewing. I still don't know for sure who I'm working for, and there were no specifics as to how and where I was to deposit you," Rone said. "I'd walk up to the castle and give you to the king, but I could get killed on the spot. You, too, if it's not obvious who you are."

"He's got a point," Farthow said, "and I'll also remind you that although you may be family with the king, there are bound to be other factions that would be happy to gain access to Catannel's favor. The Veraland Navy is still the biggest in Deideron."

"I hadn't thought of that, I just figured we'd be home free once we made it to the Northmarch," Charlotte said. She sighed.

"I don't think we'll ever be home free until Catannel's head is on a pike," Rone said. "Mark my words, he's going to far too much trouble for one woman."

"I agree, but don't worry," Farthow said. "We'll get to the pike eventually. You mark *my* words."

"Well," Charlotte said, "we found Johnny without those entrenched systems, whatever that means."

"We got lucky. Or unlucky, depending on your perspective. His skill helped us escape, but his profession as a pirate will continue to expose us to risk for as long as we're with him – and after, possibly."

"*If* he ever gets out of lock-up," Farthow said.

Rone smiled. "Yes, *if*. He's a big man, and that's a big *if*."

"Big *ifs* don't always come with big men," Farthow said.

"They do if that big *if* has to fit into a small hole."

The two men laughed.

"What are you two planning?" Charlotte said.

"Nothing," Farthow said, "Just a couple of old men from the sticks making jokes nobody understands. Why don't you two go check in with our captain? I have some… other things I have to attend to, like changing out of this uniform."

"Good idea. It doesn't suit you at all," Rone said.

"I think he looks fine," Charlotte said.

Farthow shrugged and waved as he walked away.

*

Johnny spoke quietly. "Coca, of course, is the most valuable per pound, and pretty easy to get rid of in a hurry." He was leaning against the stone wall while sitting on the mattress of the cell. The guard had given him his pipe in exchange for a piece of silver from his personal effects, and he was busy filling the room with the smoke of fresh tobacco, which drifted slowly out the long stone shafts above and out into the street.

"It's also the easiest to blow through in a good weekend," Mineo barked. The guard against the far wall continued reading his book, seemingly uninterested. "But I can show you the best way to take it, lass." He gestured to his crotch as he lay on his back.

"Is it that easy to find a buyer?" Charlotte asked, ignoring the small bald man. She leaned closer to the bars.

"It's easy to throw overboard, or into a gutter, is what I meant," he said back, closing one eye. "This really ain't the best place to buy it, either. There's always a huge mark up by the time it gets this far north. Only grows in the jungles, you know."

"It doesn't matter," Rone said. He leaned against the bars with his arms crossed. "I just need something good to sell that will turn a modest – not insane – profit."

"You mean something to sell to criminals, right?" Johnny said. "Because you could always sell a barrel of wine to the local pub when you get there."

"I need men who prefer discretion in all things," Rone said.

"Like me. Can't say I blame you. I'm famous for my discretion." Johnny said, smiling. He stood up and moved closer to Charlotte. "In Golice, like most places, there are probably a few guilds dedicated to the black markets. Items that skipped the tariff process are always a little bit profitable if a bit banal. Technology is valuable, but only to someone who understands what he's looking at, which usually means a wizard, and wizards mean entanglement with the nobility. Or apostates." He seemed to shudder. "Most of them underground sorts aren't looking to buy things like rifles and explosives, but to sell."

"Wizards? Are you serious?" Charlotte asked.

"I'm a wizard," Mineo said. "I can show you." He started to cackle slowly.

"Of course. You've never met one?" Johnny pushed his head into the bars and opened his eyes wide. "They could turn you to ash with a glance!" Johnny's face turned from grim to strangely happy.

"There are no wizards who can do all that anymore," Rone said. "It's all gone out of the world."

"Have *you* met one?" Johnny asked, raising an eyebrow at Rone, who stood statue-like with his arms crossed.

"Maybe I am one," Rone said.

"Preposterous!" Johnny said, looking away and pulling back from the bars. "Now, what were we talking about?"

"Drugs," Rone said. "By which I mean the sorts that are illicit according to either custom or law."

"Right," Johnny said. "Like I was saying, Coca and opium are always a good, profitable way to find the absolute scum of the earth. Just don't try to sell your dope to the wrong person, or-" He drew his thumb across his neck.

"Who do we sell it to in Golice?" Charlotte asked.

"I don't know." Johnny shrugged.

"You don't?" Charlotte said.

"How would I know that?" Johnny said.

"You're a smuggler?" She scratched her head in confusion.

"I'm a privateer," Johnny said.

"That doesn't include smuggling?" Charlotte said.

"Not in Golice." Johnny sat back down on the bed.

"But you smuggle things elsewhere," Charlotte said.

Johnny smiled at her and leaned back again. He drew on his pipe. "You ever hear the expression, 'Don't piss in your own pond?' My ship and its private contracts are registered in Golice."

"I'm sure we'll figure it out," Rone said to Charlotte. "I don't want to raise our profile by asking around, but I'm sure we can manage once we get there."

"How are you going to get it past the customs house and the inspector at the dock?" Johnny said.

"Kiester it!" Mineo yelled.

"Sharp ears on that one," Johnny said, staring at the little man, now sprawled on the floor of his cell.

"I figured we would use your hidden smuggling bays in the hold." Rone smiled.

Big Johnny stared at him in wonder for a moment. He closed one eye. "How did you know about those?"

"I didn't. I just assumed you had some," Rone said. "You also answered another question for me. So much for not pissing in your own pond."

"What are you smuggling?" Charlotte said.

"Bah," Johnny said. "I shouldn't tell you."

"Rifles or explosives, I would wager," Rone said. "Since he doesn't know the drug guilds."

"Those are for a royal contract, I'll have you know. Totally legal." Johnny crossed his arms.

"Not from the church's perspective. Things can get nasty

during an inquisition."

"Not like I'll be smuggling anything any time soon."

"We're working on that," Charlotte said.

"For a hefty cut of my stock." Johnny shook his head.

"I thought there were plenty of shares open now," Rone said.

"Yeah, but I hadn't planned on selling to Mitha Porthagan. Gods! I can't have her knowing what kind of things I get into."

Rone paused for a moment and looked at the ceiling. "I hope your secret is as safe with us as ours is with you."

"How secret?" Johnny said looking over at Mineo. A soft snore seemed to be emanating from him. He looked back at Rone. "You're a sly bastard I'll give you that. Coca or opium is right easy to find here. They just sell the stuff by the box at the market, though I have to warn you," he took a few puffs on his pipe, trying to bring the tobacco back to life, "if you want in the drug business you're gonna get raped on the price anywhere above the thirtieth parallel."

"We'll make this our last run, then," Rone said, smiling.

*

Though illicit materials were easy to find in the Gallow, they were located in places that indicated to some degree the danger associated with them. In the case of drugs, the most significant concentration of sellers was in Lowtown, a cluster of tenements and slums between the harbor and the western rise of modest suburbs and country shops. It was subject to flooding and to the passage and pooling of sewage from the lower quarters.

Everything there was washed in a perpetual grey; even the wooden eaves of the leaning houses had faded to a non-color from decades of neglect. Even so, there was a sense of energy emanating from the residents of the poorest quarter of the city. They guarded their old houses, swept their steps, and children played with each other in the streets, or at least the clean parts of them.

Rone walked through the dejected stalls of the market, manned by hard merchants wearing armor and carrying pikes and blunderbusses. Stacks of unprocessed coca leaves littered one stall, with a small sign hanging in front that read, "Great for a smoke- or hire your own chemist." A lean man with a short brown beard sat behind reading a small, tattered book.

"Do you know any reasonable chemists in town?" Rone asked.

"If I did, you think I would be selling the leaves?" The man didn't look up from his book. "Big mistake on the last order, this is. You can still smoke 'em to get a buzz, or chew 'em for a bit of energy, but that ain't too fashionable these days."

Rone walked on without saying goodbye. The next table had a series of tiny barrels, inconsistent with each other's shape but averaging about twelve inches in height. One was open and a well-dressed man with an outrageous purple hat, complete with a bleached white peacock plume, was bent over the table. Rone angled his head to see the man snort some of the pale powder on a metal tray up his nose. He rose quickly, rubbing face.

"Outstanding!" He said, "How much for an ounce?"

"I can do about, ah… Six argents," said a large, deeply tanned, and overweight man behind the table as he scratched his thick, black beard. Rone thought he looked Datalian.

"Splendid." The over-dressed man counted out six silver coins and handed them to the man behind the table. The dealer used a spoon to carefully measure out a pile of the white powder onto a small scale. The over-dressed man handed him a small but highly decorated wooden box. When the scale balanced, he pushed the powder into the box and fastened the lid.

"Pleasure doing business with you." The Datalian saw Rone as the rich man moved away. "What can I do you for?"

"Looking to buy." Rone walked up to the table and looked around. The fat man threw the coins into a chest, then closed it and put his foot on it.

"Of course. You want a sample, I presume," the Datalian said.

"How many ounces do you pack in one of those barrels?" Rone asked, ignoring the question.

"I don't usually sell that much around here. You looking to travel?"

"How many?"

"Two pounds plus an ounce, give or take. I don't recommend trying to sell this stuff on the street, wherever you're going, stranger."

"Why are you so concerned?"

"Don't want to sell a man his death warrant," the Datalian said.

"It's for a private party. Would that satisfy you?"

"It's your skin, son. One barrel coming up." he walked to the end of the table and picked up one of the small barrels.

"Three."

"Three? You in the business? I don't think I know you."

"That doesn't matter, and you *don't* know me. I'll give you three aurals apiece for them."

"They're worth at least four."

"Three apiece and you can buy yourself a house in this town, with enough left over for a nicer shirt."

The Datalian looked him up and down. "Alright, then. Nine aurals for the lot."

"I want to see you measure it." Rone stood still, his arms crossed in front of him.

"You're serious." The large man seemed perplexed, but

pried open a barrel anyway and began measuring it out onto the scale an ounce at a time.

*

"I don't think it would be a proper deal without opium," Rone said. He shuffled one of the small barrels to his other arm. "We'll just get a few pounds," he said, motioning for Charlotte to follow him inside the darkened house. Its porch had a leaning roof, nearly ready to collapse.

"How do you know they sell opium?" Charlotte said.

"The smell," Rone said. "Not quite so bad as the smell of it burning, but it's still there."

Charlotte puckered up her nose and did detect something rather unique, though not altogether bad. It was a wet, oily smell, almost like drying rubber.

Inside was another packed shop full of locked boxes, barrels, and other paraphernalia. There was no open guard, just a big, squat man who held a double-barreled blunderbuss lightly in one arm.

Charlotte was shocked at how expensive the strange, almost crystalline, yellow-orange substance was. Four pounds of the stuff had set her back six aurals, and all of it fit into two tiny paper-wrapped satchels. Rone hadn't bothered to haggle.

"Expensive," Charlotte said, laying the bundles inside of Rone's shoulder bag.

"It was a great price," Rone said. "We'll triple what we just paid, and the local dealers will still make another thirty percent on that. I daresay we'll have a few extra coins when we get to the end of this mess."

"As long as you're sure about this," Charlotte said.

"After all that, you're just grubbing smack dealers!" A familiar voice accosted them. They looked up the road to see Martelena Gordino stomping toward them. She had lost the innocent, sad countenance of when they had first met her and instead looked fierce and disheveled.

"Misses Gordino," Charlotte said politely.

"You probably could have bailed him out with all the money you dropped on that junk."

"It is not my obligation to do so, even if I could," Charlotte said, turning up her chin.

"You work for her, don't you?"

"Our business, whether with Mitha or not, is our own. *Stay out.*"

"You are! You're working for that whore!"

"I can see why your husband is not eager to leave the dungeon," Charlotte said.

"You're lucky I'm not carrying a gun!" Martelena moved closer to Charlotte, her hands curled into fists.

"I'm quite certain I've killed more men than you," Charlotte said. "Do not mistake a moment of mercy as weakness." Charlotte turned her back to the woman and strode away quickly. Martelena stood in the middle of the street, her jaw slack. Rone watched her for a moment, smiled at her, then turn to catch up with Charlotte.

"That was good," he said, falling into step with her. "You're becoming a regular brigand."

"It's just a conversation I didn't want to have. I'm a coward, really."

"I'm proud of you."

*

The opium was neatly packed into its own small barrel, lying under an oil cloth next to the coca and the cache of rifles onboard the now unchained Parkitees. As they left the hold, they saw the new members of the crew bustling in and out of the cabin, negotiating sleeping and storage arrangements. Pierce, the unofficial first mate turned interim captain, seemed able to settle most of these disputes amicably. Business was getting on, even if it wasn't business as usual.

The sun set in the west during Rone and Charlotte's trek uphill to Mitha's estate, casting the mostly grey city into shades of orange and red. The people they passed were all in a hurry as the clock rang out at six o'clock, broadcasting the final half-hour of business at the Gold Courthouse for the day. The men at the gate and the door of Mitha's estate were amicable, now that they recognized the pair, but there were no dinner plans; Mitha was conspicuously absent, tending to "important interpersonal matters."

Rone and Charlotte took the opportunity to recline in their bedroom, enjoying a late meal of duck and fruit brought to them by Nom the steward, as formally as ever. When they were done, Charlotte decided to seek a bath, excited to have two in as many days.

"There are two baths, dear," she said to him as she folded her white gown and placed it among her other things.

"Not to be too foul," Rone said, busing up the dishes. "but I think I shall enjoy some time to myself in the privy. The ale this afternoon doesn't seem to be agreeing with me."

"Suit yourself," Charlotte said. "I'm sure you'll be able to have one later as well." She opened up the bedroom door, and Rone stood up and rushed over to her. He grabbed her around the waist and pulled her into a hard kiss. She resisted first, in surprise, then softened to it. She opened her eyes wide as she pulled away. "What was that about?"

He looked down for a moment, then went to Charlotte's things and retrieved a pistol. "Don't forget it."

He listened for her to walk down the hall, then set to work quickly, dressing for the task ahead. He slipped on a pair of fingerless gloves, and with a ball of twine, he tied the sleeves of his faded grey shirt down tight over them. Likewise, he drew his pants and his jacket at his midsection tightly against his body. His hood lay lightly around his shoulders. His moccasins, old friends now seldom used, he slipped over his feet. They were thin and tight, and he could feel the wood floor as if he were barefoot. On top of all these clothes, he carefully put on his baggy finery and doublet. He found his wide-brimmed hat and put the ornate pen from a nearby desk in it. *Not a perfect illusion, but it'll do for now,* he thought.

The door swung open, and Charlotte slipped in. She stopped when she saw Rone standing up, fully dressed. "I... forgot to bring a robe," she said, her face cast into a frown. She still held her pistol in one hand.

"Just going to head out to get a few more supplies," Rone said, smiling weakly.

"I thought you needed to use the privy."

"Things went faster than expected."

"I'll come with you." She smiled at him. He didn't react.

"You don't need to come with me, stay here and enjoy Mitha's hospitality," he said, smiling back.

Charlotte's smile dropped. "What are you really doing, Rone? Tell me."

"I need to meet someone."

"Horseshit." She moved within an inch of his face and stared at him.

"Just-" His voice failed, and he looked away. He relaxed his shoulders. "I just need to take care of something. I was going to pack up our things and leave some instructions; I don't want to put you at risk."

"We talked about this, Rone. Putting yourself at risk puts *us* at risk. You're my bodyguard, my guide, my agent." She stopped and looked into his eyes urgently. "And I love you."

"It's nothing I can't handle," he said, shrinking from her stare.

"I'm coming with you."

"You can't. Where I'm going, you can't follow. It's something I have to do alone."

"Or nearly alone. Farthow's in on it, isn't he? I knew you two were planning something. Well, now I am, too."

X: Into the Dark

Farthow was waiting outside the gate as they appeared, dressed like a middle-class merchant and standing beside a few large sacks.

"I thought you said you were leaving her behind?" he said when he saw Charlotte wearing her fine dress with her backpack over her shoulders.

"I thought I was," Rone said.

"Here, got you some treats," Farthow said and pitched a heavy sack to Rone. Rone opened up the cinched top and looked inside, then nodded.

"So, what exactly are we planning?" Charlotte said.

"Already planned," Rone said.

"You didn't tell her?" Farthow said

"I didn't want to risk it. Mitha's walls might have ears."

"Fair is fair. I guess we can explain along the way." He smiled as he set off down the street with them.

*

The bell tolled eight times in the old clock tower overlooking the city square. Charlotte walked stiffly beside Rone, listening to him softly remind her of what she was to do. There were still many people in the square, some stopping to peruse items of necessity or convenience from the few vendors still perched about. Most of the shops were closing for the day, with the street vendors holding onto the last minutes of daylight in their little hand carts. Other groups of people were forming for social engagements at the ring of inns and pubs that faced the Gold Courthouse.

There was a little temporary textile stand that stood across from the Gold Courthouse with a cluster of women standing around it, chatting and looking over the last items remaining. Charlotte stopped a moment to look at a piece of cloth spread across a table in front. The merchant, a middle-aged bespectacled man, was busy throwing all of his bolts of fabric into his mule-drawn wagon.

"How much is this?"

"Twenty cyprals for the rest of the bolt," the vendor said, stopping his task to look at her.

"I only need two yards," she said.

"Alright, fifteen, but leave the dowel behind." She produced a few large coins from her bag, and the vendor swept them into his pocket. He finished his packing and lowered the wooden doors of the kiosk, then began to lead his mule off. Charlotte rejoined Rone as they walked by the row of vendors packing up around the perimeter of the square.

Rone walked with heavy feet. The clack of his hard heels rang out as a high-pitched snare on the flat cobblestones. Occasionally, he looked off to his left at the castle that the city called a courthouse. As they walked, one step made a low melodious tom sound, and he squeezed Charlotte's arm. They slowly turned down a narrow lane. A tall blonde man, wearing an apron, was sitting beside the entrance to a small restaurant smoking a pipe. As they approached, he looked at Charlotte and said, "Fancy a pinch and a drink? Early evening special." He nodded toward the open door. Charlotte returned the nod and walked past him.

Every few steps, Rone stepped loudly in the center of the street, his hard heels sounding out the same deep tom sound. Finally, he found what he was looking for, which was an iron grate lying flat in the street. A small amount of water flowed into it from up the hill.

"This is it," he said.

"Are you sure this is a sewer and not just for rain drainage?"

"Yes, I can smell it faintly. This is as good a chance as we've got." He looked up and down the street. The restaurateur stood with his back to them, still smoking. The street in the other direction was vacant. Rone bent down and began prying the heavy bared grill from its place using a small flattened metal bar from his bag. Charlotte looked down the street to either side. Suddenly a couple appeared from the direction of the courthouse. She recognized the man instantly as the clerk they had met outside the dungeon.

When he looked down the alley, all he saw was a middle-class woman attempting to fold a very large and unwieldy length of cloth. He looked for a moment, wondering where he had seen her face, before greeting the blonde man and walking into the little eatery. The blonde man turned around and saw Charlotte walking back up the street toward him.

"Sure you won't consider a stop in? I'll treat you if you like." He smiled widely.

"No thank you, I need to get going."

*

Rone dropped down into the sewer. He heard Charlotte push the grate above him closed. The smell, which was faint above, hit him immediately in the narrow tunnel, and he quickly stuffed his hat into his bag and tied his wet cloth around his mouth and nose. He then pulled on his hood and drew it tight onto his head. He breathed freely for a few moments, trying not to wretch. *Just a few moments, and you'll lose sensitivity to the smell,* he told himself.

He removed a small cloth bag from his larger leather one and sat it lightly, almost cautiously, on a dry brick nearby. He crouched down and began removing his outer clothes, stuffing them into his leather bag. He was left standing in his brown shirt and black pants, tied close to his body with twine in various spots. He cinched up the leather bag and slung it and the smaller bag over his shoulders.

He had to crouch to walk through the filthy tunnel. He placed his feet lightly each time to avoid the sound of splashing in the muck. In his mind, he wondered if his moccasins, aiding him in so many infiltrations in the past, would be salvageable after he dragged them through a mile of waste. *Good shoes are like a good friend. Hard to find, reliable, and hard to throw away.*

He counted his paces as he walked along, noting to himself where he passed landmarks above. *Fifty paces, restaurant. Seventy-five paces, cloth shop to my left.* He knew when he had reached the courthouse, not only by the count of his steps, but by the sewer splitting off to the right, left, and down.

Dungeon is down, he reminded himself.

Before him lay a slope so severe, it was nearly a shear drop. Slivers of dim moonlight from a sewer grate a few feet behind him cast themselves upon the smooth stone of the descending shaft. The bottom was a black abyss. He tied a rope to a loose brick protruding from the archway, tested it, and then used it to slide down into the darkness below him.

The passage he had just left seemed very dim above him, and he wondered if it was some trick of his eyes that he perceived light at all. He reached out and touched the wall and felt his way, as near as he could tell, north toward where he reckoned the dungeon to be. He hoped that the careful memories he had made when visiting Johny would lead him true.

He still had his small oil lamp, as well as some extra matches in his pocket he could use if he got desperate, but he wasn't there yet. He needed to save those things for later.

Rone's senses began to sharpen as he went down.

The passage went on until he felt it open to his left and perceived a dim light in that direction. He followed it. Suddenly, the light grew bright, and he squinted, trying to rectify it with the darkness of the last few minutes. About twenty paces away, he could see firelight being cast down into the sewer through a grate. He could hear a sloshing sound as waste temporarily blocked out the light, falling in front of him. He had grown used to the smell of the sewer, but fresh remnants carried their own stink, and he stifled a cough. He crawled to just in front of the grate and listened to a few voices.

"How does it feel to dump out my shit?" a familiar voice said.

"It feels like being a free man, earning coin," a voice said back. "Thank you for at least crapping in the bucket. You don't know how many people here shit all over the floor thinking I'll come in and clean it up."

"Haha! You don't?" said the first voice.

"Not until they're dead, which means I got the last laugh, or they've paid up, and we *do* charge extra for soiling the cells."

"What is there to eat today?"

"Same shit as always."

Rone pulled from a pocket a small mirror attached to a thick copper rod. He pulled on the rod, and it extended as a series of small nesting metal tubes, like the barrels of a tiny spyglass. He pushed it up through the bars of the grate and saw in it a reflection of the small dungeon lit by dim lamps and candles. The first voice belonged to, he could now verify, Mineo Gordino, who hung his arms out of the bars of his cell as another man, short and slouching with wispy grey hair on the top of his head, pushed a plate of no-colored slop under a gap in the bars.

"Shit food, shit company, shitty shit," Mineo said, picking

up the plate and shoveling the food into his mouth.

"I'm the only company you get. You really ought to be nicer to me. If you break my heart, I might forget to feed you or empty your bucket."

"Bah, I've got this fat chap at the end to talk to," Mineo said, gesturing behind himself. Rone turned the mirror and could faintly see Johnny at the other end of the room, sitting on his mattress and eating quietly.

"He'll be out tomorrow," the old man said. "One way or the other."

"They hanging you, boss?" Mineo said to Johnny.

Johnny looked up. "Not tomorrow. Maybe the next day. Maybe the judges will side with me and set me free."

"What are you in for?" Mineo said. "Can't have been too bad, I saw your lawyers."

"He's got lawyers?" the old man said.

"Yeah," Mineo said. "And one of them's a girl, a right pretty young one. I bet she's got a scut to kill for too. Nice and tight."

"Oh, I *wish* she were here," Johnny said with a laugh.

"Me too," Mineo said. "I'd grease her up with some of this slop and tend to her back door, if you catch my meaning."

"You're disgusting," the old man said. "How'd you ever get a woman to marry you?"

"Doing what I just said," Mineo said. "You got to find the right type. The kind that like it up the arse will do just about anything for you, and like it."

"Actually, I changed my mind," Johnny said. "I wish the other lawyer was here."

"I figured he was more your speed," Mineo said. "You being a sailor and all. I bet he's got a big dick, too, to fill an arse like yours."

"Because he would cut your tongue out," Johnny said.

"That's something, Minny," the old man said. "You're so filthy you're making the sailor blush!"

"What happened to the other fella that was in here?" Mineo asked. "The big ugly southern dandy?"

"Francis?" The old man scratched his head. "Got sold as bond for his debt. They sent him down to market in Masala."

"Shit," Mineo said. "He was at least interesting to talk to."

"Did he have soft hands?" the old man asked.

"What the fuck is that supposed to mean?" Mineo said.

"Ha! Nothing, 'cept what you think. I'd miss him too if I were a man like you. You ain't the only sailor in the room." The old man blew Mineo a kiss. He sat down at a little table right above the grate and across from the small group of cells and began eating a hunk of cheese.

Rone thought about how he could throw a weighted garrote around the man's neck at that moment and have himself light, likely the keys, and if not those, all the time he needed to pick a lock. That would be a loss of life, though and would defeat part of the point of his little mission. *It was so much simpler back then,* he thought to himself, shaking his head.

"I swear Jim when I get out of here-" Mineo began.

"You'll what?" the old man interrupted. "You'll thank your lucky stars somebody bought out your worthless maggoty ass. Gods know I wouldn't spare a penny for an old cheat like you."

"Fuck you, Jim."

"I know it's not going to do you well, being cooped up in there alone without poor Francis to reach through the bars and help you relax."

Mineo pushed the cleaned plate forcefully through the bottom of his cell door. Jim got up and picked up the plate, then walked down the row and picked up Johnny's. He pulled the lamp off the wall on his way back, then banged three times on the steel door at the far side of the room. A guard opened a small window at the top, looked in, then Rone heard the bolts sliding before the door opened outward.

"See you tomorrow, renegade," Jim said mockingly. "Do avoid breaking your neck trying to suck your own cock while I'm gone, I'd hate to be out of a job."

So that jailor doesn't carry keys at all, Rone thought.

The light from the torch faded as Jim walked away, and the door closed, leaving the little prison almost totally dark. The only light was the small beams that escaped through the edge of the door or the peep-hole. Rone waited a few minutes, leaning himself against the sharp bricks that lined the tunnel to take the tension off his thigh muscles. Mineo began to whistle in the darkness.

Bah! This creature never shuts up.

Rone leaned up and looked through the small bars of the sewer. Mineo was directly across from him, laying back-down in his cell again. He could see Johnny far down at the other end. He had misremembered where the sewer grate was, and he realized he would be unable from where he was to pass Johnny the pieces of equipment necessary to free him. Rone sighed.

"Mineo," Rone whispered. Mineo continued his whistling etude. "Mineo," Rone said again, rasping. The etude evolved into a sonata, the melody floating high and modulating freely. "Mineo Gordino, shut the fuck up!" Rone said at last, bringing his voice into tone. Mineo stopped.

"Johnny, can you hear me?" Rone said, unable to see Johnny's cell without the help of the mirror.

"I can now," Johnny said. "What are you doing here?"

"Who's there?" Mineo said aloud.

"Quiet!" Rone whispered. "I'm here to get you out. Both of you, I guess."

"Really?" Mineo said aloud, then whispered, "Really?"

"Yeah." Rone thought quickly. "Your wife couldn't get your stocks sold, so I'm going to break you out of here."

"So, she found out they're all junk huh? Shit," Mineo said. "Where are you?"

"I'm in the sewer," Rone said.

Mineo snorted. "You know you're standing in my shit, mate."

Maybe I should think about this some more, Rone thought.

Rone removed from his pocket a small open-wick oil lamp made of brass. He opened up the top and felt the soaked wick, then spun a little rough wheel pushed by springs onto a small section of flint. Sparks leapt up, but the wick didn't catch fire. He tried a few more times, but still, the lamp did not spring to life.

Rone heard a snap and felt an empty spot where the flint was supposed to sit.

"Hold on," he said aloud.

He crouched down, into the recent muck, and felt around for the fallen flint. He had to suppress a gag several times, but for all his searching with his bare fingers, he could not seem to find the flint.

He withdrew his pistol from his bag, quickly emptied the pan into the sewer, and tried to use its flint on the wheel of the little lamp. Sparks flew, but again, it did not light. Rone rechecked the contraption. He grunted aloud when realized that the wick was indeed soaked, but with water as well as oil. Somehow, he had not kept it dry on the way to the courthouse dungeon.

Rone took a deep breath, wiped his fingers carefully on a spot of his pants, then fished in a pocket. He found his few extra matches there, and they felt dry enough to use. He stood back up and, by the dim light of the dungeon, struck the first match. It erupted and died without bringing the wood of the matchstick to life.

Rone tried another. This one caught flame, but died before he could get the wick hot enough to light while wet.

The next match didn't spark. A dud.

He had one last match. He held it up in front of his face. It was just barely visible. "Of course my plan hinges on one thing that cannot seem to work, and I'm losing all the time in the world."

"What?" Mineo said.

"Dreamer, if ever you indeed hear prayers in your realm beyond time, let this one work," Rone whispered.

He struck the match, and it came to life. Quickly and carefully, Rone put it up to the wick. He could almost see the fibers beginning to light when the flame began to die.

"Please," Rone said, concentrating all his thought on the single match, now just a strand of tiny warm coals. "Please," he whispered again.

As if hearing his wish, or perhaps responding to the rush of air across the hot wood, the match caught fire again, then the wick hissed and caught light.

"Thanks," Rone said. He pushed the lamp through the grate and looked around again with his mirror in the flickering light. Johnny was standing at the end of the row, squinting. Rone checked the sides of the grate and determined the old iron was indeed set in the stone. He grabbed the bars and tested them. They rattled slightly, but the mortar was still holding firm.

"You here to break me out or just give me a little light?" Mineo whispered.

"Patience, son," Rone said. "You will need the light in a moment. I need you to do exactly as I say."

"Trusting strangers standing in piss and shit? Why the fuck

not?"

"What do you need me to do?" Johnny whispered.

"Hold on for a minute." Rone pushed a small cylinder through the bars and held it on the floor with tense fingers. "Mineo, I'm going to try to roll this toward you. I need you to catch it. Be careful with it. Okay?"

"Okay," Mineo said.

Rone pushed on the small cylinder, and the tension of his fingers launched it toward Mineo's cell. It bounced on a few uneven places on the floor then clanged against the bottom of the cell door. Rone held his breath.

"Got it. Hey, what is this?" Mineo said. He shook it next to his ear.

"For the sake of the Dreamer don't shake it, it's explosive," Rone said. Mineo held it away from himself and eyed it suspiciously. "Roll it down the way to Johnny."

"You gonna blow the lock?" Johnny said.

"That's the idea," Rone said.

"Why should that bastard get out and not me?" Mineo said.

"I have another one for you," Rone said. "Just roll that one down to Johnny, coordination is critical."

"Fine," Mineo said. Rone peered down the lane between the cells as Mineo reached through the bars and rolled the cylinder down toward Johnny. It bounced about tremendously from the pitch, and Rone held a gasp, but Johnny was able to reach through his cell door and retrieve it.

"Get ready for the other one," Rone said. He pulled the second cylinder, which Farthow had purchased as a back-up, out the bag, and repeated what he did with the first. Mineo caught it before it hit the bars this time.

"What do I do with it?" Mineo said.

"There is a lid on it, carefully unscrew it," Rone said.

Mineo unscrewed the container, and another smaller brown cylinder, a tiny knife, a few matches, and a fuse fell out. Johnny did the same. "Do you know where the keyhole to your cell door is?"

"Of course," Johnny said.

"Not in the dark," Mineo said.

"You've been here over a month, and you still don't know where the locks are?" Rone reached down for a minute and rubbed his forehead. *This man was a smuggler?* "Find it!"

"Okay, I think I found it," Mineo said.

"Check to see if the explosive fits," Rone said.

"Which one's the explosive?" Mineo whispered.

"The one that isn't the knife, match or fuse." Rone began to sweat, his frustration bringing forth what the warm rot of the sewer could not.

"Okay," Mineo said.

"Aright, I need you to use the knife to poke a hole in the top. Put the fuse in. Make sure the stiff end of the fuse goes in first."

"Okay," Mineo said.

"Got it," Johnny said.

"Put it in the keyhole of the lock," Rone said.

"Done," Johnny said.

"It doesn't fit," Mineo said.

"Why didn't you tell me?" Rone whispered angrily.

"You only told me to check. You didn't tell me it needed to fit."

"Hold on. Someone's coming. Hide that stuff!" Rone pulled his small lamp back down into the sewer and Mineo dove onto the bedroll, hiding the small explosive beneath himself. Johnny quickly pocketed the cylinder and matches, then leaned against his mattress.

XI: Down and Out

Charlotte walked calmly, along with the few remaining people in the square, toward High Town. Occasionally, she could feel the clink of metal in her bag or feel a hard bulge bump against her leg. She smoked a small meerschaum pipe Farthow had handed her. It was the type she knew to be fashionable with ladies of the middle class in Veraland. Smoking was, however, a habit that for women had not permeated the Northmarch, and she was unaccustomed to the techniques involved, coughing harshly whenever she drew in a bit too much smoke. She did her best to stifle these impulses, wanting to draw as little attention to herself as possible.

She saw the shop she was told to look for after Rone dropped down into the sewer. The nursery had closed and locked its shutters, and the lights inside were out. The rows of plants on the large patio were now gone, save for a few exotic potted palms that were too large for a thief without a wagon to abscond with. She quietly reached into her bag and felt for the bomb with the next shortest fuse. She pulled out the heavy iron ball and touched the fuse to her lit pipe. She carefully pushed it into one of the palm pots, its fuse glowing and burning down slowly.

One to go, then to turn back when the action happens. She turned the last corner and saw the back door to Doughan's pub. She pulled the final iron bomb out of her bag, lit the fuse and threw it casually into a barrel standing a few feet from the door, then turned quickly and walked back in the direction of the Gold Courthouse, nervous sweat beading her face.

*

The peephole of the door opened, casting pale torchlight into the little prison. A guard put his face up to it.

"You asleep already Mineo? I ain't been hearing you whistle, you alright?" The guard said, peering in.

"I was asleep. Now I'm awake, thanks to you," Mineo said. A low-pitched boom sounded through the lockup.

"Hey sarge, you gotta get up here!" A voice said from behind the guard. Sounds of footsteps could be heard beyond the door.

"Go to sleep! Both of you!" The Guard slammed the peephole shut.

"What's going on?" Mineo whispered.

"Our diversion. Now, we need to hurry!" Rone put the little lamp back up. "Use the knife to shave down the sides of the explosive. Try to cut as little off as possible. And be careful, or it could explode and kill you." Mineo kneeled and began shaving down the little stick. Johnny already had his in the lock. "Hurry up!"

"I'm going as fast as I can, considering I could die at any moment from this shit," Mineo said.

"Die in here or on stage. Your choice." Rone busied himself with his own explosives. He set a few more of the sticks in the stone around the grate, inserting into each a fuse. He held them against the bars in a few places with balls of wet clay.

"Okay," Mineo said.

"Did you put it in the lock?"

"Of course," Mineo said.

"Johnny?" Rone said.

"Ready to go when you are, lad," Johnny said.

"Okay, get ready to light the fuse. Once you light it, back as far away from the door as possible. And cover your face."

Mineo struck a match. It quickly died. Rone held his breath, looking over to see Johnny cradling a small, burning match. Mineo struck another. Sparks leapt out from the fuse. Rone didn't have time to see if Johnny followed suit. He quickly held up the flame of the lamp and lit his own. He dropped back down into the sewer and scrambled behind a bend. He put his fingers in his ears.

A few seconds later, the first explosive detonated, tearing apart the lock on Mineo's cell and flinging the steel door open. The second occurred, and the barred door to Johnny's cell flung itself against the wall, clanging loud enough to match the sound of the explosions. Then the sewer grate was obliterated, along with all the stone surrounding it. Rone dashed back down the tunnel and began pulling rocks away, holding his lamp in one hand. The room was dense with smoke, like an impenetrable fog.

"Get it in here, you fools!" Rone screamed, no longer caring about stealth.

"What did you say?" Mineo called back, staggering through the smoke.

Drat, I forgot to tell the idiot to plug his ears! Rone said. He stood up in the room and gestured for Mineo to follow him down.

"Why aren't we going out the door?" Mineo said, pointing down the length of the dungeon.

"Because there are guards that way!"

"What?!" Mineo swayed in confusion.

Johnny appeared out of the smoke and grabbed Mineo by the collar. "Just follow the man, gods!" He marched both of them to the smoking sewer entrance and threw Mineo into the darkness before getting on his back and sliding in himself.

Big Johnny, having to stay nearly bent to the floor to stop his head from being knocked about by errant stones, kept a hand on Mineo's back as he followed Rone down the low-ceilinged sewer way. He tried desperately to get the smuggler to move beyond a plodding stagger, but Minneo was tottering like a drunk goat. Finally, Rone stopped at an intersection and lit another fuse with his small lamp. He wildly exaggerated the motion of putting his fingers in his ears and Mineo, finally understanding, imitated him. Another explosion rocked the stone as the sewer behind them collapsed.

*

Charlotte nearly fell with sudden fear as the first bomb went off, rocking the back wall of the courthouse. She fell in step with a group of people running out of the restaurants and public houses to see the commotion. Some looked frightened, others merely curious, and many now held arms. The small herd, gaining members as it went downhill, was flushing the onlookers down to the back of the square and the Gold Courthouse.

She saw a group of guards assemble outside the front door of the fortress-like building, looking confused. She slid past the other people, working her way over to them, and cried out.

"The back of the building, somebody was using a bomb at the back of the building!"

Without discussion of the strange woman's sudden appearance, the guards barked to each other quickly.

"The vault! Get Sarge up here, you two walk around to see what's happening," the leader for the moment yelled to the others. Two of the men jogged off, one holding his halberd at the ready and the other clutching a blunderbuss. Charlotte slipped back into the mass of bodies and began jogging against the crowd in the direction of where Rone had entered the sewer. A minute or so later, the next bomb exploded, lighting the awning of the nursery on fire.

Please be alright. Please! she thought.

Mineo and Johnny followed Rone down a few twists and turns until they finally reached Rone's rope. Rone pointed upward and handed the rope to Mineo. The fat sailor tugged on it, trying to pull himself up, but was never able to get his elbows past a slight bend.

Too weak and too fat to climb a rope. How this man was a sailor I will never know, Rone thought to himself. Johnny grabbed the man's legs and began to push up, groaning with the effort. Mineo made it a few feet past the shoulders of Johnny, and then the rope snapped the stone protrusion to which it was tied, causing Mineo to tumble down onto Johnny.

"Son of a Bitch!" Johnny said, pushing the fat man off of him. The rope fell limply at their feet. Mineo looked over and shrugged.

"How are we supposed to get out now?" Rone said. He clenched his hands into fists and hit his temples with them.

"I don't know. You didn't think of this?" Mineo said.

"I devised an exit route. I didn't, however, take *you* into account," Rone said.

"What's that supposed to mean?" Mineo's face, for the first time, took on an appearance of offense.

Rone threw up his hands. "A fat, foul-mouthed, ungrateful, idiotic, sailor who can't climb a damn rope!"

"I wasn't sure who you were talking about there for a minute," Johnny said, rubbing his back as he staggered to his feet.

"Yeah, why would you expect a sailor to have a clean mouth?" Mineo said.

"Now we're trapped down here," Rone said.

"No, we're not," Mineo said.

"Eh," Johnny said. "I've seen worse places to die."

"We're not trapped," Mineo seemed calm, even

nonchalant.

"I'm not sure I have," Rone said to Johnny. "I'd prefer for the last thing I smell to be wildflowers, not shit."

"Fellas," Mineo said. "We're not trapped."

"You know a way out?" Rone said.

"The sewers empty into the ocean, we can just go out that way," Mineo said.

"Of course," Johnny said. "Why didn't you just say that?"

"You didn't ask," Mineo said.

"How do we find our way there?" Rone said. "These shit-pipes aren't exactly easy to navigate. I don't even know which way is North."

"It's easy, you walk downhill. You aren't very bright, are you?" Mineo put his hands on his hips. Rone squeezed his hands into fists again but controlled the urge to hit him. A cacophony of footsteps and voices sounded out above them. Rone pulled a small roll of paper from his bag and wrote on it quickly with a piece of charcoal he produced from inside his glove. "I thought we needed to hurry," Mineo said.

Ignoring him, Rone finished, rolled up the paper, and tied a small piece of twine around it. He jumped against the wall and pushed off, propelling himself upward. He managed just to reach a small grate, about the size of his head, and push the roll of paper into it before tumbling to the ground. He landed hard and felt a sharp pain in his ankle. He bent down to feel it for a moment.

"Nice trick," Johnny said. He reached up high and felt to the same opening with his hand. "How about next time you just ask for a little help?"

Rone laughed. For some reason, at the bottom of a waste-filled tunnel in the darkness, surrounded by enemies, it seemed like the funniest thing he could imagine. He bent over, took a breath, then motioned both of them to follow. They dashed down the way they came, Rone's little lamp casting light in front of them.

*

Charlotte waited above the grate. There was still a frantic crowd in the center of the city, and a person would occasionally go running past her in either direction. As they did, she would move down one lane of the intersection or the other, hoping to seem innocuous. No guards had made their way up to where she was. Rone had yet to emerge from the appointed sewer grate, and the street was quiet. As time plodded forward, she began to wonder if it was because Rone had already been caught at the courthouse.

In the silence of the night, the worry began to nag at her, and her imagination invented many endings to the story, none of which were pleasing. A terrible sense of loneliness crept into her, along with a dread that it was she that had crafted Rone's doom. *If I had left it alone – if I never put my foot out that door – he would be safe and in my arms.* She took a deep breath, buried her fear, and put her worry aside.

The minutes ticked by as the noise from the square began to die down. A couple of young men, carrying muskets but dressed plainly otherwise, appeared around the corner, meandering up toward her.

"Yar, those explosions were for real," the shorter of the two said. "I can't tell what they was trying to hit, or if they had some kind of vendetta against the whole square."

"Ted's nursery is wrecked," the other said in a deep voice.

"Nah, all the plants are inside. His awning's ruined, though, and those palms were worth a few argents."

"Yeah, good thinking of him. Do you think they were really trying to get in the vault?"

"Who knows? Nobody's ever gotten in before. Don't see how that should change now." The shorter of the two noticed

Charlotte standing in front of him. "Evening ma'am. You waiting for someone?"

"My husband heard some noise from the square and went down to check on our shop," she said.

"Oh yeah?" the shorter man replied. "Which shop is yours?"

Charlotte's brain raced. "My husband sells… textiles, just off the square proper."

"Oh, so you're Gunter's wife?" The short man cracked a wide smile through his young but stubbled face. "I never knew that bloke was married. Funny how the little things slip by. Our uncle Samuel runs a gun shop next door. He sent us down there to see what's up."

"Is everything alright?" She asked.

"Things are dying down. Your shop is fine. Courthouse guards are bloody serious about something, though," the shorter man said again.

"Then if you'll excuse me, I need to see to my husband."

"Sure thing. Tell Gunter I said hello!" The pair continued walking up the lane as Charlotte rushed past them, pulling up her skirt to free her feet.

I will not suffer despair without a look for myself, she thought.

Around the corner, Farthow appeared, dressed plainly. She ran toward him.

"He's not at the other grate," Farthow said, "though I think I've drawn the guards away from this one."

"He's not here either," Charlotte said, swallowing hard.

*

After what seemed like hours stumbling through the dark of the tight and twisting sewer, they came upon a widening of the tunnels. There was there even a semblance of light, though it seemed to illuminate nothing but the sheen of the muck surrounding their feet. The arched tunnel would have been big enough for all of them to run, but the very slippery substances underfoot demanded a more cautious approach. The opening of the sewer way also meant a slowing of the passage of waste, and Rone's mask, soaked in water before to deaden the stench, was now drying out at the same time the sewer contents were piling up. He held his little lamp aloft, but the floor seemed to be little more than wet blackness. *Probably better if I don't see it,* he thought to himself, trying not to choke from the smell.

Mineo staggered next to him, pushed along by Johnny's massive hands, which picked him back up whenever he stumbled. Rone was sure he would have vomited, had there been anything left in his stomach to throw up. As it was, only an occasional hack or gag would escape him. After a few minutes in the broader tunnel, the dim light started to become substantial and less of an illusion bleached out by Rone's small hand lamp. At last, in the distance, they could see pale glow bleeding between the bars of a large vertical grate. Rone quickened his pace, allowing Mineo and Johnny to fall behind for the moment. Beyond the tunnel's exit was another silvery reflection, rippling and moving chaotically – the ocean.

The end of the tunnel was closed off by an iron gate, rusty and overgrown with green slime. A heavy chain, slightly less rusted, was wrapped around the gate's closure and the surrounding iron bars. A padlock hung down on the outside, gently rapping against the iron bars as the wind howled outside. Past the gate was a small stone ledge, and a narrow stairway leading up to the right, looking as ancient as the gate itself. Beyond the shelf, all that was visible was the ocean in the cove, gathering the moonlight in many small waves.

Rone reached through the bars and grasped the padlock, testing it to see if it was both locked and secure. The lock wouldn't budge. He stepped up and felt the hinges of the gate, which were caked in rust. He rattled the gate door, hoping that the inclusions of rust would break the old hinge, but it stood fast. When he stopped, he heard the rattle echoing loudly down the corridor behind him, and he became suddenly aware of the silence he was disturbing. He pulled the padlock in past the bars and examined it carefully.

Mineo, huffing and staggering, jogged up behind him, Johnny close behind. "What's the problem?" His voice echoed loudly.

"Shhhh!" Rone hissed. That sound echoed too. "Keep your voice down, the open end of this tunnel is amplifying us," he whispered.

Mineo looked over Rone's shoulder. "Why don't you just blow it up like we did on the last lock?" he said quietly.

"I don't have any more explosives."

"Any gunpowder?"

"Yes, but we're whispering for a reason," Rone said. "By now, they've realized you're both missing and that you went out the sewer. They might be inclined to look for us here." Rone pulled a small flat canvas satchel from his pocket and unfolded it on a nearby stone. Inside were a variety of steel implements.

"What are those?" Mineo asked.

"Tools of the trade," Johnny said, watching Rone.

Rone selected a piece of flat metal and small tension rod, curved at the end, and began working on the lock. He felt the tumblers and springs through the tips of his pick, working carefully and swiftly. After just a few moments, each tumbler was locked in place, and he turned the whole mechanism. The lock fell open, and Rone replaced his tools. He set the padlock down silently and began removing the chain, doing his best to be stealthy, though the clinking of the many links on the old iron bars was unavoidable.

At last, the chain was off. The gate began to move in response to a hard push. The ancient and rusty hinges began to squeal loudly, and Rone winced at their report. He tucked his tools back into the long pocket of his pants and stepped out onto the windy precipice, feeling sudden relief from the oppressive smell of the sewer. Mineo and Johnny (ducking under the low arch) followed him out to the small ledge.

The wind, mighty at the top of the cliff, blew up under Rone's hood and scattered Johnny's hair around wildly. Below them was a great fall, ending in spires of twisted rock a few dozen feet below them. When Rone poked his head over the edge, the crashing of the waves against these sharp teeth grew to a roar. He became aware that the sound of the sea was nearly non-existent in the small tunnel, and he wondered if anyone about would have been able to hear them anyway. The moon was visible, still rising barely above the outcropping that surrounded the tunnel's exit, some ten feet higher than the ledge.

"So, we're facing west," Rone said. "The harbor will be south of here, then."

Rone pulled the gate closed and started wrapping the chain back through the bars.

"Why are you doing that?" Mineo asked, no longer whispering.

"Never hurts to cover your tracks; keep people guessing as to where you've been and when. Besides, what if someone was following through the sewers, eh?" Rone clamped the lock back onto the chain and started up the old crumbling stair. As he reached the top, he stopped in his tracks, his head just poking above the level masonry above the sewer exit. Two men sat on the crumbling stones about ten feet from the landing, their backs to Rone. In front of them was a waning campfire they had built in a dry gutter. The pair were sitting close together to shield the flames from the wind off the ocean.

Sparse houses and stone buildings, all with darkened windows and ill-tended yards, littered the landscape behind them. The two men wore steel breastplates and simple helms, and each had a blue feather protruding from it, like the guards from the little jail. As they talked to each other, one fidgeted with a blunderbuss. The other leaned on a long halberd.

"What is it?" Mineo asked. Rone quickly reached down and put his hand over the former prisoner's mouth. Johnny peeked up his head cautiously, and Rone looked down to see the sailor standing a few steps below him. The two men at the fire continued, oblivious, and Rone realized that he was holding his breath. Mineo inched himself around Rone, taking in the view for himself.

"That captain I understand. Men will stick up for their captain in a pinch, but why would anyone bust old Mineo out of jail?" one asked.

"Don't know, he don't have many friends. I would think it would be a fine... ah," the other man snapped his fingers then pointed at the first. "Diversion. Yeah. This is when I'd try to bust the vault. You know, if I were a thief."

"There's no way to break into that vault anyhow unless you were a wizard or something."

"There are wizards in the world. Somebody managed to break the prison all apart. I bet a wizard had a hand in it."

"Yeah, but they didn't bust the door, did they? And the one in the vault is twice as big and thrice as thick." The guard took off his helm and wiped his face with a rag, then replaced it. "I don't think we'll see the old bastard or the captain again."

"You mean we're wasting our time out here?"

"Better than working." They both laughed.

Mineo ducked back down and whispered to Rone and Johnny, "The one on the left is Hitch. The stupid one on the right is named Mel. They're both right cruel."

"They were fine to me," Johnny said.

"You weren't there long enough to get hungry," Mineo said. Rone looked at the man's gut, which spilled over his worn belt. "You got a wire or knife? We can off 'em real quick and get out of here."

"We're not killing them," Rone said.

"Why? I thought you were trying to help me escape."

"We are – I am," he corrected himself. "But nobody dies tonight." Rone turned around and looked over the edge again, watching the waves beat against the rocks.

"Whoa, lad, you're not thinking of jumping, are you?" Johnny said.

"We might have to," Rone said, silently counting the waves, waiting for a large one to cover the rocks.

"You're stupider than you look," Mineo said. "Let's at least try to sneak by."

Rone took a breath to calm himself. "Alright." He stood up slowly and silently walked to the top of the stair again. Hitch and Mel seemed to be enjoying each other's company still. Johnny, despite his size, seemed limber and capable of stealth. Mineo was the variable, and Rone wondered if the clumsy man would be able to tread silently even in the wind. Rone crept to the landing and motioned Mineo and Johnny to follow. He spied a line of bushes running behind a house to their right, and without any other options, began to make his way to it, moving slowly behind the guards.

XII: The Business

Panic began to set into Charlotte's throat, clogging her breath and spinning her head as her heart raced. She walked briskly back toward the grate Rone had used to enter the sewer, suddenly fearing that he had emerged and found her absent. She tripped suddenly and almost fell, sliding her feet apart on the smooth stone and flinging her hands out for balance. Farthow caught her from behind, leaving her face pointed at the rough cobblestones. With her head hanging downward, she saw something.

"What's this?" she said to herself, bending down to the little gutter.

"Sorry, what?" Farthow asked.

In between the bars of the grate, no more than six inches tall, sat a small piece of paper, with a small knot of twine around it. Charlotte unrolled the little bit of paper and read it.

"I'll never curse luck again when I trip!" She handed the note to Farthow, who read it quickly.

"He's going out a different way," he said. "Where the sewer empties. The cove to the East."

Charlotte picked up her skirts and hurried toward the harbor, Farthow following closely.

*

Rone focused on his body, relaxing what he could while he held his foot aloft, though his muscles resisted with a rigid tension. He set his toe down, slowly transferring his weight to it as it came to rest fully on the ground. In his mind, Rone wondered why he was bothering, given Mineo, who probably had as little practice in sneaking and stalking as he did running blockades. Then there was Johnny, whose weight was as likely to crack the old paving stones as not, no matter how softly he tread.

Still, it's best not to double up the noise, Rone thought. One of the men from the courthouse threw another small twig on the little fire.

"Can't wait for summer to get here. Cold down here at night," Mel said. "And my jack ain't too good for staying warm."

"It's cold up here in the summer too. Sea wind does that. Even the people who can own a house don't want one up here." Hitch took his helmet off and set it down, then began scratching his scalp and scraggly beard. "Dry sweat is the worst."

Rone continued tip-toeing across the patchy grass toward the line of wild bushes, Mineo behind him and Johnny in the rear. He heard a crack and turned back to find Mineo frozen, his foot pressing down on a wooden piece of debris. The men continued talking.

"You should really think about a rag under that helmet," Mel said. Rone continued tip-toeing.

"But then it doesn't fit as well. The leather's already too thick."

"I swear I get a rash on my forehead without a rag on my-" Mel suddenly stopped. Rone looked over to see the man looking back at him from the reflection of Hitch's shiny helmet. Mel turned quickly, and without even standing up, swung his halberd in a wide angle toward Rone. Rone jumped and looked down to see the blur of the steel spearhead under his feet. Mel was on his feet quickly, and Hitch was scrambling for his blunderbuss. Mineo stood shocked, his eyes open as wide as a fish's. Johnny rushed past him.

Rone dove to his left and missed another swinging strike from Mel, just as Johnny approached from behind, reaching under the man's arms and pressing his palms to the back of the guard's head, locking both of his shoulder joints. Hitch shouldered his heavy blunderbuss and cranked back the overlarge hammer, leveling the muzzle at Mineo. Rone, breaking out of a roll, kicked the gun at the stock, knocking it into Hitch's chin. The muzzle fell forward as Hitch dropped the gun barrel-first into the dirt. A few small balls of shot rolled out of the end of the gun as Rone stood up and pushed Mineo back onto the stairs. He reached for the familiar handle of his sword and felt a twinge of panic when he realized he had left it wrapped up and sticking out of his bag. His pistol, likewise, was still stowe.

Mel, unable to free his arms from Johnny's nelson, pushed the blunt end of his pole between his legs, let go, then kicked the butt of the halberd up into Johnny's crotch. The captain staggered back, winded from the strike, then fell onto his back, his head hanging over the edge of the masonry, just as Mel picked his weapon back up.

Rone dodged a quick stab from Mel's halberd and turned to see Hitch picking his gun up again. "Johnny, the stairs!" he yelled. Johnny groaned in reply and rolled himself down the first stairs, his belt buckle rattling on the old stone.

Ignoring the stairs and the large man blocking them, Rone dove over the side of the cliff, feeling debris and rocks kick into his feet and legs as the blunderbuss roared, flinging dirt up from where Rone had just been standing. He landed on Mineo, and both of them nearly fell over the edge. They scrambled up quickly.

"I guess it's the ocean after all," Rone said. "No time to count."

"Son of a bitch," Johnny groaned, pulling himself off the

bottom stairs and struggling to stand.

"Just jump," Rone shouted.

"What?" Mineo reeled in confusion as Rone grabbed his collar and threw him over the edge. Rone looked down to see him splash just past the rocks. He turned to Johnny, who pushed away his grip and jumped half-heartedly off the precipice, stumbling at the end, which sent his arms flailing as he tumbled. Rone looked over to see another splash. *Thank the dreamer,* he thought, then turned to see Mel coming down the stairs, his halberd held out as far as his grip would allow.

Rone turned back to the sea, took a deep breath, and leapt. His thoughts raced during the descent, and it seemed as though he had a long time to ponder many things while the shiny blackness below slowly moved up toward him.

He considered whether he should try to enter on a slim profile, feet first, or slow his landing on his back. *Feet first. I could break a bone from this height on the water, whether there's rock below or not.* He considered how he could get back to safety. *Swim. Nothing for it.* He wondered if he had lived a good life. *I can do better.* His last thought filled him with a fear of death, something he had not experienced in a long time. He splashed down, feeling his body plunge into black water. He felt his feet hit a boulder below him, the hard, sharp shells of barnacles tearing the bottom of his moccasins. As he bent his knees to pad the blow, he felt one of the carapaces scrape through the leather and into his right foot painfully. He pushed off and held his breath, swimming forward and trying to get back to the turbulent surface at the same time.

His head emerged, and he took a deep breath. He looked around for Mineo, who was frantically trying to keep his head above water and reach the rocks. *He can't swim either. Why should I be surprised?*

"We'd best get on with it, lad," Johnny said. Rone turned

around to see the tall sailor's head bobbing a dozen paces beyond him. "There's still a gun up there!"

He looked up to the ledge above him to see the two men, now rather small figures in the pale moonlight, looking down at the water. He realized the rocks on the south end of the tiny bay they had leapt into were in the shadow of the moon's light, and there might be hope in avoiding sight. He swam over toward Mineo, putting his arm around his chest and pulling him away from the rocks with a strong scissor kick. Johnny watched him and followed his line, swimming laterally toward the shadow of the cliff.

"Got to stay away from the rocks, we'll get battered to death there!" Rone shouted into Mineo's ear. Mineo coughed and sputtered in response. Rone pulled him through the shadow, hoping that they were unseen by the men above. He thought that Hitch would have reloaded by now, and though the blunderbuss had little in terms of range, he knew a stray piece of shot could still hurt. After a few dozen feet, Mineo began to relax and kick a little bit with Rone.

The three of them exited the shadow and began swimming in the moonlight around a large outcropping of rock that enclosed the southern portion of the small cove. Rone paused and put his hand to his ear, but was unable to hear any report of the two men over the sound of the ocean. Southward there ran a long stretch of rocky shore, and Rone wondered where he'd be able to pull Mineo back onto land. His legs were already getting tired, and his foot was stinging and burning.

"Gonna be a long swim," Johnny shouted over the banging of the waves on the rocks.

"Longer for me than for you," Rone said back.

"Let me know if you need some help with the lubber," Johnny said.

Mineo gargled in protest, his voice croaking as if he was

trying to speak.

"I will," Rone said, kicking hard to try to catch up to Johnny as they pushed their way out of the rising humps of the waves. "Are you hurt?"

"Getting kicked in the balls fills you with all kinds of feelings," Johhny said. "Your back hurts, you need to shit… but I'll live. You?"

"Think I sprained an ankle and cut open the other foot," Rone said. "Luckily, we're not having to run anywhere right now."

"How bad is the cut?" Johnny said.

"I can't see," Rone said. "It hurts pretty bad. Why?"

"Just thinking about sharks," Johnny said.

*

Pierce was drunk. Charlotte had found him inside Johnny's quarters, looking over manifests and leaving the rest of the crew outside to drink grog, the removal of the ships impoundment (by an iron chain) having driven the crew to celebration even in the absence of their captain (*or perhaps because of it,* Charlotte thought).

It seemed impossible to explain to pierce the situation. His response to each statement was things like, "The bloke is in jail!" and he only became fully cognizant of her intent as she and Farthow attempted to push the longboat off the main deck.

Once he realized what they were doing, he was quick to join them but slow to give any real help. The boat was in the water before he started to give instructions on how to manage the pullies that launched the craft.

Pierce handled the ropes and rudder well enough, but he seemed to mumble curses constantly. Charlotte sat at the bow, still in her dress, looking out around the shore as they carefully worked their way north. Unlike most companion boats, the boat for the Parkitees, nicknamed "Bertha" by the crew, was more than a lifeboat with a few oars. It had a small mast, which could be removed and laid flat while it was on the ship, a rudder, and a sail. Pierce, despite his stupor, was still able to rig the sail, and it currently sat across the mast at an angle catching a crosswind.

"Where are we going again?" Pierce asked, leaning on the rudder and looking slightly sick as the waves bobbed the boat up and down.

"We're looking for the exit to a sewer," Charlotte said.

"Just follow the shore around north and east," Farthow said. "Could be a cave or a drain, or-"

"Or a river of shit, eh?" Pierce laughed and took another swig from a whiskey bottle he had refused to leave behind.

A flash of something white in the distance made Charlotte stop and squint. "Do you have a glass?"

"I'm not sharing. Get your own whiskey!" Pierce said, smiling broadly.

"I meant a spyglass," Charlotte said.

"I have one," Farthow said and pulled a brass-barreled spyglass from his inner jacket pocket. Charlotte looked out in the distance as she extended the objective and saw the white splash again. She quickly held the glass up to her eye and focused the image. Charlotte saw another small splash, then a whitecap with two heads coming up from it. She could see arms waving. Great, big, long arms. *Johnny*, she thought. Looking past him, she could see a wet hood attached to a swimmer that seemed to be having a hard time swimming. Struggling beside him was a man that was bald, his head a white dot in the moonlight. As she focused, she realized that it had to be Mineo.

"Over there!" She said, pointing to a cluster of sharp rocks.

Pierce straightened up and squinted. "Can't sail in there.

Wind gets funny in a little cove like that."

"Then row."

"Why don't you?"

"A lady doesn't row." She crossed her arms.

"A lady doesn't dig convicts out of the sewer, either." Pierce laughed at himself.

"One of those is your captain," Charlotte said.

"Yeah, and I'm liable to get it," Pierce said and took a sip of whiskey.

"I'll row," Farthow said, pulling up the pitted wooden oars from the bottom of the boat.

"Sounds good to me." Pierce yanked on a rope and pulled up the sail. "I'll man the rudder."

"You realize we don't need it with the oars, right?" Farthow said, looking over his shoulders as he dipped them into the water.

Pierce stared off for a minute. "I knew that."

*

Rone found that Keeping Mineo afloat was a monstrous challenge, despite taking turns with Johnny. His legs ached, and Mineo was no longer able to help propel them. He seemed surprisingly un-buoyant in the saltwater. He felt the man pull him down, and both their heads dipped below the waves. Rone kicked furiously to bring them up again.

"Just lay on your back!" Rone shouted at the near-drowning man next to him.

"I can't," Mineo gasped. "I'll sink!"

"No, you won't!" They dipped below the waves again, and Rone suddenly felt devoid of strength. He considered letting Mineo go but was pulled up by a pair of large hands before he could give it more than a fleeting thought. Johnny now swam beside him, tugging one of Mineo's arms while Rone dragged on the other.

Exhaustion was setting in, and each kick was slower than the last. Rone turned his head and was able to look in front of them with one eye. He saw a boat and began to panic. Treading water, he looked for a place he could drag his burden, but rocks and the plumes of angry waves were all he could see.

"We might have to leave him," Rone said.

Johnny ignored him and continued to move forward. Rone relented and pushed onward, giving his best effort to help the captain with Minneo.

"Rone! Johnny! Can you hear me?" a familiar voice said, barely above the hissing of the sea. Rone turned to look at the boat and saw a slender body on the bow, and long hair, a dark grey in the moonlight. He felt a return of hope and began kicking furiously toward the boat. As it approached, he could recognize Charlotte's familiar profile, though her face was in shadow. Johnny and Rone reached the boat at the same time, and Charlotte reached over and grabbed each of their free arms as they touched the side.

"Never mind us," Johnny said. "Get this poor sod here off of me." Johnny dragged Mineo again by the collar, up toward the boat. The drowning man seemed to get some life back into himself, though he coughed still, and latched onto the side. The boat began to tip toward him.

"Whoa, don't knock us over!" Pierce instinctively fell against the opposite bout.

"With Pierce," Farthow said, moving to the side and grabbing ahold of Mineo. He strained but failed to lift the fat man even half-way out of the water.

"Hold on a minute," Rone said, turning loose of Mineo and swimming to the other side. He reached into the water and slung a wet bag onto the little deck and grabbed the side with both hands. "Come here, Charlotte." Charlotte moved over to help him. "Don't worry about me. Don't let go, Mineo!" The boat was now tipping toward Rone. "Pierce, get over there and pull him up! Johnny, you push the bastard out."

"I'm the captain, I thought I was supposed to give the orders," Johnny said.

"Then just do whatever the hell you want," Rone said.

"Fine." Johnny ducked below the water and grabbed hold of Mineo's legs. He began kicking hard, pushing the man up as Farthow and Pierce pulled up on one of his arms each. Mineo man finally tumbled over the side of the boat. It rocked a few times, then slowly settled. He gasped as if he had never breathed before.

"Ok, don't move, stay on that side," Rone said. He tensed his tired back muscles and pulled himself up and out of the water, turned his palms onto the railing and pushed himself all the way up, so his waist was against the upper edge of the boat. Rone wearily pulled one leg into the boat, then the other, which were heavy with wet cloth. He sighed. "Let's get Johnny up."

"If there's one thing I can do, it's get in a boat," Johnny said. He was working his way up the other side, resting on his folded arms and trying to push his body the rest of the way in. "Little help," he said grunting. Farthow grabbed the collar of Johnny's shirt and pulled. When Johnny flopped into the middle of the deck, the large boat dipped in the water wildly from port to starboard.

"Gods, the smell!" Pierce said, scrunching up his face.

"Sorry, I had hoped the water would have washed most of it off. Some seems to have stuck," Rone said, lying down and dropping his head to the deck in a sudden need for rest.

Charlotte smiled. "And now you've got it all over my nice dress." Charlotte looked at the gasping sailors, who didn't seem to react. She sighed and moved above Rone, pushing his wet hair out of his face. "You must be tired."

"I just dragged a fat man through a mile and a half of ocean," Rone said. "A surprisingly unbuoyant fat man. I'm ready for anything."

"Always with the sarcasm. At least I know you're alright," Charlotte said.

"And no sharks," Johnny said, poking at Rone. "You're a lucky charm, even if you're a heap of bad luck."

Charlotte smiled and looked into Rone's eyes. "I'm a little disappointed, though. You said nothing about how sailors shouldn't complain about the smell of ass, or that you're surprised he can smell anything through the whiskey-"

"My whiskey!" Johnny said, seeing the bottle rolling around up near the rudder. He dove toward it, rocking the boat, and held it up in the moonlight. Only a small amount remained at the bottom.

"Aw, you spilled it!" Pierce said.

"You been drinking my highland sweets," Johnny said, holding the bottle to his chest and pointing at Pierce . "There will be consequences for this, mark my words!" He quickly started drinking down what remained before choking. He dropped the bottle, and Pierce picked it up and finished it off, then gave a grunt.

"What's wrong?" Charlotte moved over to Johnny as he coughed violently.

"It was seawater!" He leaned over the side of the boat and vomited suddenly. One the other side, Pierce looked like he would do the same, but was perhaps held back only by how little he had swallowed.

"Must have gotten filled in all the rocking," Pierce said, and groaned painfully.

Farthow inched himself up on his elbows to watch. "I guess I'll be rowing us back as well."

"I'll row," Charlotte said.

Pierce held his head above the side for a moment, still fighting the vomit. "I thought you said," he coughed, "That ladies don't row?" He leaned back over the side and started retching.

"I can do it, I guess. I still have a little more powder in the horn," Rone said, sitting up.

"Sit down." Charlotte put her hand on Rone's chest and pushed him down onto the bench seat on the bow side of the mast.

"I'm fine rowing. It's a good back workout," Farthow said, using one of the paddles to try to bring the boat about. "We'll be back in the wind in no time."

They moved out into the open water and turned the boat south. Charlotte and Rone loosed the drawn sail and let the cross-wind pull them back toward the harbor.

"Thank you," Mineo said, looking up at Charlotte as she looped the rope around itself. He looked tired and humble, more like the man in the guillotine and less like the man making lewd comments in the prison.

"I didn't do anything. Well, except save your life just now." She sat down and held onto the rudder. "I guess that *is* quite a bit. You're welcome, though you should thank Rone."

"I get the feeling he didn't care much for getting me out," Mineo said.

"I still don't care much," Rone said.

"Well I don't give a *shit* for getting you out!" Johnny said, suddenly roused from his stupor. His scowl broke into a strange smile, and he laughed.

Rone joined in the laugher. "But all the same, I guess I feel alright about it. It can be my good deed for the week." He sat down and began shivering as he finally noticed the cold wind blowing through his wet clothes. "I think every shirt I own is wet now. And my poor shoes," he looked down at his moccasins, cut to ribbons and hanging in tatters from his feet.

"What happened to your foot!" Charlotte said, pulling his leg up and wiping away the blood and torn leather on his sole.

"Damn Barnacles. At least I cut my foot in the water and not in the sewer," Rone said.

"I'm telling you, I'm damn shocked we didn't attract sharks," Johnny said.

"They don't come out at night," Mineo said.

"Damn, son, you *are* a lubber," Johnny said. "Sharks are always sharks. They never sleep. In fact, if they stop swimming, they die."

While Charlotte began tying the wound with a make-shift bandage, Rone opened his bag and looked at the clothes Charlotte had bought him in Masala, which he had worn over his current gear, to see if they had survived the sewer. He had managed to keep them clean, but they were soaked with seawater.

As if sensing his thoughts, Charlotte said, "We're going straight to the ship now, so you won't need them to sneak around town." She wrapped her arms around Rone, pulling him into the heat of her body, ignoring the smell.

"Tell me," Mineo said, still lying down. "What was the explosive we used to break the lock and bars in the dungeon?"

"I forgot," Rone said.

"Bullshit."

"What does it matter?" Rone asked.

"It wasn't gunpowder. I know that much," Mineo cast an odd glare at them as if he was a thief studying a mark.

"He's a wizard, you know!" Johnny leaned against the side of the boat. He looked cheerful despite the stains of vomit on his grey shirt.

"Just another tool of the trade." Rone cracked a slight

smile.

Farthow laughed. "It is indeed. I hope you stocked up."

"What trade?" Mineo cocked an excited half-smile.

"We just call it the business," Farthow said. Rone joined him in laughter.

Sitting in the boat with Charlotte's arms wrapped around him and a free wind in his face, Rone knew he could no longer call it merely "business."

XIII: Shoals

Rone and Charlotte watched as Pierce and a few deckhands pulled Bertha back onto the starboard side of the mid-deck using the pulleys. Other sailors dashed between the forecastle and mast, trying to prepare the sails while still more (many with grog in hand) hauled supplies up from the dock. Preparations were being made for a swift departure, as it was plain that the operators of the Gold Courthouse would eventually remember that one of the fugitives had a ship at dock. Johnny sent a lone runner to gather up what could be found of the crew off-ship before disappearing into his quarters, cursing about the smell of the sewer.

"What do we do with him now?" Charlotte asked quietly to Rone as she nodded toward Mineo. He lay against a rail with a cup of grog, his soaked beard dripping beneath a deep scowl.

Rone sat on a box, carefully removing the tattered remains of his moccasins and his torn shirt, shivering in the sea breeze. "Is that our responsibility? We saved him from execution; he can find his own way now."

"Can he stay in town? I would think he would get locked up again as soon as he was found. Too bad Fathow's already gone."

"I don't think Farthow would have the time or inclination to keep him safe. It's up to Mineo where he goes now. We certainly can't take him with us."

"We could. We could get Johnny to hire him as a hand. We

can't just save him, then leave him to die."

"That is a terrible idea," Rone said. "The man is weak as a noodle and heavy as clay, and he can't swim. He's a terrible sailor; how he managed to command a vessel is beyond me. And I don't think he endeared himself to our dear captain during the escape."

"I suppose you are right. It's not our responsibility anymore, is it?"

"It wasn't ours to begin with. We've done more than our good deed for the week."

"Oh Rone, your foot is much worse than you led on," Charlotte said, bending down and picking up the now naked sole. In the lamplight, she could finally see the long, jagged gash that ran down the arch of his foot to his heel. Fresh blood was there, weeping out as she squeezed the wound shut.

"Ah! What are you doing, woman?"

"I think we're going to have to stitch it up. It's wide."

Rone pulled his foot up with some effort to look at the wound. He gave a slightly disgusted look. "I think you're right." He grimaced as he pulled at the skin to examine the inside.

"I'll see who in the crew has some experience with surgery." Charlotte stood up and looked around at the chaos.

"I can do it myself if you just fetch me a needle and thread."

"You've impressed me enough already today," Charlotte said. "You don't have to sew your own flesh up to make me think you're more of a man."

"It's not that," Rone said. "I just don't trust-"

Charlotte didn't listen to the rest, but ran off toward Johnny's cabin, dragging her wet skirts behind her.

She returned a few moments later with Johnny himself, who was shirtless, his hair sticking out in wild directions from the water and wind.

"Mate, you're in great luck," he said, pulling up Rone's foot to look at the sole. Rone winced as he poked near the wound. "Good and clean, I say. No reason to heat up a poker."

"I said I could do it myself," Rone said.

"Let's get you inside where I can see better." Johnny grabbed two nearby crew members, and they helped him pick up Rone and shuffle him over to the captain's quarters, where they plopped him down in one of the chairs.

"You've done this?" Charlotte said.

Johnny moved quickly about the cabin, grabbing various items. "You don't run a warship without learning a thing or two about treating injuries. Light another lamp, will you? I want to see what I'm doing."

"Any more whiskey?" Rone said. "To clean the wound."

Johnny laughed at him. "I always keep a few extra bottles of the good stuff around. Hopefully, Pierce didn't loot my whole stock. Not the best behaved first mate I've had."

"Certainly not the worst," Rone said. "If I remember Masala right."

Johnny's face went downcast for a moment. "Aye, Danny. He was a good lad, till the end there. No matter, I *do* have some." Johnny reached into some hidden space behind his bed and retrieved a large corked bottle of nearly clear liquid. "I keep the good stuff hidden well enough, I suppose."

Johnny pulled up Rone's foot and, ignoring all the wincing from his patient, doused the wound with water and booze, and then cleaned out the clots and scabs with a coarse bandana.

"Do you have to be so rough?" Charlotte said.

"He's a tough bastard," Johnny said. "Most men are crying for their mum about now." He pushed harder into the wound with the cloth, removing more clots, then doused the wound again. The liquor brought up fresh blood, which Johnny wiped away quickly with another rag. "Besides, quicker is better. More pain for less time is always a bit more tolerable than the other way around. You ever have an itch you can't scratch?"

"Charlotte," Rone grunted. "In your bag is my medicine satchel. Do you remember what it looks like?"

"No."

"I haven't used it since the mountains. It's black, about the size of two hands. Fetch it, please."

"Alright," Charlotte said. "Is that it?"

"We'll need hot water, too."

"I have a stove here," Johnny said.

"I'll be right back," Charlotte said and stepped out the door.

"Good thinking," Johnny said. "No reason a lady should have to watch this."

Rone nodded, and Johnny threaded a large, curved needle. "Best to be accurate rather than quick, captain."

Johnny smiled. "I'm both."

He had finished the ugly business by the time Charlotte returned. Though there were still spots of weeping blood, but the wound was closed and his foot looked otherwise whole.

"This is it, I think," Charlotte said, and handed Rone the small bag.

Inside were numerous small vials and pockets filled with dried herbs.

"If you had opium in there, we probably should have started with that," Johnny said, washing his hands and arms in a nearby basin.

"No opium in here. We do have a few pounds hidden in the hold, though," Rone said. "This is just old medicine."

"Magic?" Johnny said with a raised eyebrow.

"Maybe," Rone said with a chuckle. "But if so, it's weak. In the old days, you could brew a potion that would close the worst wounds of battle or chase away deadly poison. Now? Well, we'll see."

"Feel free to use my stove," Johnny said. "I need to get this ship out to sea. Now, I think. They'll eventually look for me here, and I'd like to be gone when they do."

"Mitha's men know a way out. I'm not sure which ones, though."

"I'll figure it out," Johnny said. He pulled a jacket from a pile of clothes near his desk and threw it around his bare barrel-chest. "And thanks for getting me out."

"I'm the reason you were there."

"Right," Johnny said, pausing at the door. "I guess you owe me double, then, Ha!"

He walked out and slammed the door behind him. Even through the dense wood, Rone and Charlotte could hear him barking orders frantically.

Rone hopped over to another chair by Johnny's small stove. It was a cast-iron piece clearly meant to do little more than heat up water for tea or coffee. Rone dipped out a cup from the water barrel nearby, then put it onto the stove. Using the flame from a lamp, he lit the few pieces of coal in the bottom chamber. When the coals began to smoke, he opened up the flue on the iron stack leading outside.

Charlotte pulled a chair beside him and laid the medicine parcel out on his lap.

"Are you serious about the magic?" Charlotte said.

"For now, I'm just trying to dull the pain a bit." The cabin rocked slightly. "We're shoving off. Good." Rone began holding some of the vials up to the light, inspecting their contents, then using a small silver measuring spoon to put tiny portions of the substances into the water. He hesitated on one vial, full of a fine brown powder.

"What's that?"

"Something precious. And dangerous."

"A kind of drug?"

Rone shrugged. He sighed and carefully put in a few grains. He closed his eyes and began mumbling as he stirred it all into the steaming water.

When he stopped muttering, Charlotte said, "Prayer?"

"In a way," Rone said. "An incantation. A memory."

"Of what?"

"The prim," Rone said. "The fathomless infinity that we are all born from - that this *world* was made from." He sighed again. He tapped the side of his head. "Everything has become so straight, we've almost lost it, but it's still there, in our memories."

"You talked like this before, in the mountains. When you healed me of my fever."

"What do you remember?"

"You and me."

"I mean, what did you remember when the fever was on you, and I gave you the medicine?"

"The same. You and me, but we were different." Charlotte leaned against him as he steadily stirred and began to mutter softly again. "We lived there, in that little house. We were married. We had a daughter."

"Is that why you love me?" He began incanting again.

Charlotte was silent for a few moments. "I feel like there has never been a moment when I didn't love you. It's like a dream I can't remember, or can only remember pieces of, where you weren't a stranger. We always knew each other. Always loved each other."

Rone stopped stirring and picked up the cup of hot water. The inside had a strange, semi-translucent color of orange that gathered the light around it. He blew the steam off the top and waited a moment.

"It sounds like madness, doesn't it?" Charlotte said.

"It sounds that way," Rone said. "But I believe it." He took a sip of the potion. "I believe it," he repeated. "Vindrel and I always had one profound disagreement – that the Dreamer existed. He's a follower of the gods, now. Your twelve gods. Ever have I rejected them as false upstarts, but my faith in the true god of eternity is rather new, I realize." He took a deep drought of the potion. "This magic is real, however small. This world is not yet totally mundane, at least. I can feel it, can you?"

"I don't… I don't know."

"We're touching a kind of dream." He shook his head. "The way it should have been. I'm so wicked, Charlotte. How can you love me?"

Charlotte reached forward and touched Rone's smooth face, where tears were starting to form in his eyes. "All *I* know is a good man."

"I love you. Dreamer help me, I do, and I can't figure out what to do about it."

"Just take me forward," Charlotte said. She looked around. "How will we get you out of here when you can't walk?"

Rone swallowed the rest of the potion. "Just give me a few minutes. Then the pain will be gone, and I'll be able to move a bit."

*

Rone hobbled out of the cabin, helped only a little by Charlotte, who couldn't reasonably take much of his weight on her shoulders. The Parkitees had already cleared the docks, and the deckhands were busy trying to rig the sails to get her moving in earnest. Rone collapsed onto a crate near the stairs up to the poop.

"Where are we going?" he shouted.

Big Johnny's face appeared over the top rail. "Not that

way," he said, pointing to starboard.

Even in the dead night, Rone could see the dots of lights and the great shadows of ships floating out past the shallows.

"Mitha's man knows a way around them," Johnny said. "Why don't you head down to the quarters and take it easy? We've got this."

"I'd miss all the action."

"Action is what I aim to avoid."

"All the same."

"Suit yourself, but I'd take a wink if I were you."

Rone shook his head. "Charlotte, can you fetch my boots?"

"No."

"What?" Rone said, shooting her an incredulous look.

"You're staying off of that foot."

"I don't think that's up to you."

"I can still go throw them into the ocean. Now let me take you down to bed. You need to rest."

"I don't think so."

"I do."

"Are you going to drag me there?"

Charlotte gave him a cold look, then stomped away.

"Mighty Nautus, what did you say to her?" Johnny said, stepping past him as he went down the stairs and back toward the captain's cabin.

"I told her I loved her," Rone said.

Johnny laughed. "Bad move. Now she owns you, you poor bastard."

All Rone could do was shake his head in reply.

Charlotte did return a minute or so later with a thick wool blanket, which she draped around Rone.

"There, now at least you and your stubborn..." Her face scrunched up, then she said with some effort, "*Arse* won't get chill."

Rone laughed.

"Laugh all you want," Charlotte said. She tried to hold a stern face, but a smile slipped in for a moment. "Now *I'm* going to go change. Don't get any ideas about sneaking in to peek at me."

She turned away, stopped halfway down the deck, nearly causing a sailor to bowl her over, looked back once, then went on.

The ship leaned to port for a few seconds, then righted. They were indeed not heading out to sea, but to the cove and the cliffs that hemmed edged the city. Rone pulled the blanket more tightly around himself as the wind kicked up, running slightly cross to the deck. The ship slowly turned to a few barrier islands near the cove. A lighthouse was perched on some rocks in the distance.

Johnny re-emerged with a spyglass, cursing softly to himself, but smiling.

"Problem?" Rone said.

"No, not really, just a bit… Nervous, I suppose."

"I'm nervous, too, if that is any consolation."

"Eh, you're always too cool on things," Johnny said. "I got a feeling this isn't going to work."

"What's the plan?"

"We're going to cut through the shoals. Apparently, there is a dip in them that is just deep enough to get a ship along, if the wind is good enough. Mitha's man," Johnny thrust a thumb over his shoulder toward the wheel, "Jasonick says he's done it before. The tide is still a little low, but he says we can make it."

"You trust him?"

"I don't see any reason he would wreck a ship he's on," Johnny said. "But still… I've had this ship a long time. Say a prayer, won't you? To whatever god you follow. One of them has got to be listening."

Johnny padded back up top. Rone watched the shadows of the Veraland fleet as the Parkitees picked up speed. It ran straight north, far closer to the mottled cliffs of Tyrant's Gallow than any ship of such size should be able to manage, but somehow it sailed on. They got so close to the cliffs at one point that Rone could hear the waves breaking on the rocks and could feel the wind off the cliffs buffeting the ship, making one or another of the sails snap.

"Kill the lights!" Johnny shouted. Crewman rushed around and extinguished the few lamps, leaving only the waxing moon to light the deck.

They entered a narrow way, between two jagged rock formations a hundred yards from shore. The ship cleared them with ease, then Rone, standing to see ahead, spied the actual danger.

The lighthouse was closer now, but Rone could see it sat on a narrow island. The white foam of the waves revealed a series of shoals, some just below the water, that stretched between the island and shore, as well as between several other rocky islets, sticking up like old stumps.

"They're signaling!" A voice said. Rone looked up to see one of the new crewmen leaning out of the crow's nest. He stood, wincing on his injured foot and looking over starboard. Several of the ships in the distance were now using light signals, flashing large lanterns toward one another.

"Let them," Johnny said. "We'll be far out of range of any pursuit soon enough. If we don't wreck my poor ship."

Rone was so focused on the signals, trying to make sense of their almost familiar code, that he didn't notice charlotte sneak up behind him.

"I found a few dry effects for you," she said.

Rone turned to look at her and smiled. "Thanks. And my boots?"

Charlotte frowned and licked her lips. "I'll help you inside so you can change."

Just then, the lighthouse went dark.

"A little help from our friends!" Johnny shouted. "Easy!"

"I'll change in a moment," Rone said, limping up toward the forecastle. "We might have a shipwreck right now. Then I'm going to want my feet bare." Rone ascended the stair, using the rail to stay off of his injured foot.

"What is that?" Charlotte said when she reached the top.

"Just wait."

The sails went taught, and the ship rocked as the rudder worked against the momentum, turning the ship a little to their right. The bow shot up a moment, then crashed back down, sending water spraying up over the rails. Charlotte grabbed hold of Rone for support, and he, in turn, held onto one of the rigging dowels that was near at hand. A few idle sailors had the same idea as them and had come up top. They cheered as the spray enveloped them.

The ship leaned to starboard and made a small but desperate turn. The bow went up again as the Parkitees buffeted against a buried shoal, then the floor vibrated as the bottom of the hull scrapped something. The momentum was strong enough, however, and the bow crashed down again with anther spectacular splash. The ship lurched and repeated its bob one last time before beginning to even out.

The ship was now in full sail. The barrier islands were further away from the big island's shore, which was also now lower and made of beaches of dark sand, almost shiny in the wet moonlight. The Parkitees had made its escape. It was now separated from its enemies by distance as well as line of sight.

Rone hobbled back down the stairs. He could no longer

see anything beyond the barrier islands besides the infinite night.

"This is just how I like it to be," Johnny said to him. He had returned to the main deck and was sitting on a stool, looking cheerful and tired at the same time as he packed a pipe. "The wind at our back and the ocean in front of us."

"There's also a couple of hundred guns at our backs, too, captain," Rone said.

"If they saw us."

"I'm sure they did."

"If they can find us," Johnny said. He put the pipe in his teeth and felt in the pockets of his jacket, looking for a match.

"They'll certainly try."

"Captain... Is that the pipe you had with you in jail?" Charlotte said.

"Of course," Johnny said, smiling. "I wouldn't leave one my truest possessions behind."

"I was just thinking about where it's been," Charlotte said. She gave Johnny an apologetic, open-faced smile.

Johnny frowned and took the pipe out of his teeth. He looked at it almost scornfully before craning his head around. "Pierce! I have a present for you!"

"I have one," Charlotte said and removed the pipe she had tried to smoke earlier in the night from one of her trouser pockets. "I've never gotten the hang of it."

"Thank you," Johnny said, taking the small meerschaum pipe. "I'll give it back, as long as you won't be needing it."

"It was Farthow's as far as I know. I can always steal Rone's if I wish."

Rone chuckled. He looked at Charlotte. "I think I will get off of this foot and have a rest after all. The medicine is not sitting well, and the sea is not helping matters."

"Are you alright?"

"I think I will be. Just need to close my eyes for a few minutes, that's all."

*

Rone watched the shore. It seemed to be changing. Slowly and subtly, the beaches and rock formations moved. The shape of the land shifted. As he watched, he realized he was on a hill that was growing. It was covered in green grass. The wind rolled over it, and he saw that the grass was moving like the water. Waves began in the infinite bright blue below him, then continued over the grass to where he stood.

He turned from the Ocean and saw a vast, empty plain, with a forest in the distance. It began as suddenly as the water ended with wet sand, and like the shore, it changed its shape slowly. Rone began to realize that if he focused on one area, or one tree, that focus of his vision would remain fixed, but he could see the other shapes changing in his peripheral vision.

There was a hill above him now, he realized, that had grown up when he wasn't looking. At the top of it was a tree. Feeling an impulse to go to it, he began walking.

He winced. The pain in his foot was nearly unbearable. He focused on the pain, and it intensified. He couldn't stop walking, though, and so he continued plodding up the hill, grunting against the pain in his foot. The pain got worse with each step until he reached the shade of the tree.

It was a massive thing, reminding him of a yew, but it twisted away in all directions with many large trunks like an ancient oak. As he collapsed, he realized he was hot, and the shade gave him relief.

He looked down at his bare foot to see a jagged and ugly stitched-up wound there. He reached down and touched it lightly. It was tender, pulsing with pain wherever he touched it.

"What? Who is it this time?"

Rone pushed himself back up to his feet, looking around

himself quickly to see to whom the raspy voice belonged.

"Above you, silly!"

Rone looked up to see an exceptionally large raven perched on a tree limb above him. It appraised him with a cocking head and dark, intelligent eyes.

"Who are you?" Rone said.

"I asked first."

"I suppose you did. Why should I tell you?"

"Because I can turn you to ash, is that a good enough reason?"

"You?"

"No, dummy, my friend the dragon. Of course, me!"

"How?"

"Don't tempt me, silly creature. Now tell me your name!"

Rone looked around at the empty plains surrounding him. "Where am I?"

The raven laughed. "Where? Where?! You really are quite dull, but… Perhaps you are not dull, just silly. Since you won't give me a name, I'm going to call you… hmn, yes… let's see…"

"My name is Rone."

The raven hopped down from its perch, landing on the turf. It began to hop around Rone, rocking and laughing. "Too late!" it said. "I have already named you Juxtatopicaladad!"

"It doesn't work that way."

"In my tree, it does."

"I'm not *in* your tree. I'm below it."

The raven hopped up on one of the lowest branches, sitting at eye-level with Rone. "Juxtatopicaladad the fool. An excellent name. My name is Zald."

"What is this place?"

"Ah, that's a better question. Getting some idea yet?"

"I'm dreaming, aren't I?"

"Yes, and so am I."

Rone eased himself back down to the ground. "I don't remember you, I'm sorry."

"I would be offended, Juxtatopicaladad, but I don't remember you either."

"Am I dead? I don't remember how I got this." Rone pointed to his wound. "Maybe it went bad and killed me."

The bird stood still, seeming to contemplate him with his unknowable black eyes. "No, not dead. Why don't you get rid of that scratch, eh?"

Rone stared back at the bird. "How?"

"Too long away, methinks," Zald said. "You can't remember that either?"

Rone shrugged. "If I ever knew." He stared at his wound for a few moments, then back up at the bird. "How is this tree here?"

"It's my tree, so it's always here." The raven gave a strange croak, almost like it was sighing. It hopped down to the ground. "You have the spark, just focus. It should be easy."

"I don't-"

"Bah!" Zald interrupted. "Let it never be said I am unkind, especially to Juxtatopicaladad." The bird hopped onto Rone's thigh, then leaned down as if to inspect the wound. It rocked and breathed out. Rone flinched as he saw fire seem to leap from the raven's open beak.

The bird flapped back up into the tree. "Yes, Zald is ever merciful, especially to Juxtatopicaladad."

Rone looked down at his foot. The wound was gone, and in its place was no scar or deformity. It was as if his foot had never been hurt.

"Thank you," he said.

"Bah, thanks are for nothing. You owe me a fresh kill. You are a mankiller, yes?"

Rone tried to remember exactly who and what he was. He looked up at the Raven. "I'm a damn good one."

"Well, you owe me a meal. A fresh, dead, man. Yes! Both eyes! Be ready to give it up."

Rone laughed. "You'll have to come and collect it."

"I will. Ah, but we have made a bond, oh unwitting Juxtatopicaladad, the fool." The raven cackled maniacally. "And a bond I shall indeed hold you to. Farewell!"

The huge bird flew off from the tree into the sunlight. As it flew away, it seemed to grow rather than diminish in size.

XIV: Greyskins

Rone opened his eyes. Though the cabin was dark, there was enough light leaking in around him to confirm that day had come.

He made to sit up but found that he couldn't. He looked to his left and saw that Charlotte was lying against him, her head on his arm, which was numb. He tried to pull it away without waking her, but she woke up as soon as he moved it an inch, shooting up off the bed and flailing her arms about as if searching for something.

"It's just me," Rone said. She paused and looked at him in surprise, her hair a wild tangle of red hiding most of her face. "I appreciate you looking for your pistol, though." The night before began to come back to him.

Rone swung his legs out and stood up without thinking. He walked across the room to where his backsword hung with his belt. He picked it up and slid it out, then smiled as he saw no rust. There was only a few beads of errant water unable to find the steel through the coating of tallow he had put on it. He shook the water off, then turned over the scabbard, shaking out a few more drops of water.

"Rone," Charlotte said, standing up and trying to smooth out her hair.

Rone looked at her and saw that she was wearing only her white shift. He smiled.

"Your foot," she said, walking over to him.

He picked up his foot and looked at his arch. A long, thin thread weaved its way through his skin, but the wound was closed. Not just closed – it looked almost like the wound had never been. Only the thread and a narrow pink scar gave a hint as to what had been there. He laughed in amazement, put down his sword, and sat on the small bed. He pulled his foot up higher.

"It looks better," she said.

"Not just better," Rone said. "Almost totally healed." Rone got a small knife from his pack and cut the knot on the thread. With a grunt, he tried to pull the stitching clean of his skin. It wouldn't budge. "Well, this presents a challenge."

"Here," Charlotte said. She took his knife and carefully cut one of the stitches, then, with some effort, pulled the small length of thread through the skin. It came out bloodstained.

Rone took a deep breath.

"Did that hurt?"

"Very uncomfortable," Rone said.

Charlotte continued until she had removed all the thread a piece at a time. Rone wiggled his toes. A few drops of fresh blood collected in some places, which he wiped away with a cloth.

"I guess that medicine really was magic," Charlotte said.

Rone turned his head to her, frowning contemplatively. "Maybe. Maybe it was something else that was magic."

"What do you mean?"

"I had a dream. I met a raven…" He shook his head and laughed softly. "Impossible to explain. I think it was like your dream in the mountains. Something divine…" Rone frowned. "My people once held such dreams as sacred, but I think we'll have to consider it later. There's a lot of moving feet outside."

*

Rone quickly understood the sudden motion of the crew. A pervasive tension hung on the men of the Parkitees because several ships were trailing them.

Rone hopped up to the poop deck and found Johnny there with Pierce and a dark-skinned man dressed in a grey wool jacket and tricornered hat.

"I guess we didn't slip them," Rone said.

"No, but in open water, they'll have a hard time catching us," Johnny said.

"The ships of the line, maybe," said the dark-skinned man. "But that's not all they have."

"Jasonick?" Rone said.

The dark-skinned man nodded to him. "They've been gaining slowly since dawn. There's three, it looks like."

Rone scratched his chin, itching already with the first of his beard re-growing. "Might want to have anyone with marine experience get their guns out."

"We have plenty," Jasonick said. "All of us have *some* experience in battle."

"I hope it don't come to that," Johnny said, pushing back his hat to scratch his oily head. His eyes looked worn and almost swollen. "But we best be prepared. I'll go unlock the stuff."

"Unlock?" Rone asked.

"I know better than to leave my precious arms unattended when I walk ashore," Johnny said. "And a good thing I did, too, considering the party of drunk sailors we had on the ship last night."

"I was going to ask what you intended to do about that," Rone said.

"You'd earn a lashing for a comment like that on the wrong ship, lad," Johnny said with a smile.

"Oh, I know it," Rone said.

"I'll worry about dockings once we get clear of that fleet." Johnny nodded off to the southwest, at the shadows floating in the water.

"How's the cannon on this ship?" Jasonick said.

"Thirty-four guns, some six pounds, some eight. We also have a gun we call the long nine we like to fire off the bow."

"Are you sure you're in the business of taking prize? That's an awfully weak complement." Rone said.

"It ain't how many you load, it's how you use 'em," Johnny said. "The Parkitees, when properly manned, is quite a force to be reckoned with, I'll have you know."

"It had better be," Rone said. "They're fast out there, but don't think they aren't carrying a sizeable number of canons and marines."

*

By midday, the ships had gained a considerable amount of water on the Parkitees. There were now three in full pursuit, a lead ship that was larger than the other two but riding high in the water. A fourth ship, larger than the others, had fallen back and was now almost out of sight.

Johnny sat smoking in a wooden chair near the wheel, which a very hung-over Pierce held steady. The captain held his hat low, but his bloodshot eyes were open in a stare that was determined to deny his need for rest. He nursed a cup of coffee, long gone cold.

"Take a look for me, won't ya?" Johnny said Rone, holding up his telescope. "Looking across miles of water whilst on a bobbing ship doesn't sound too fancy to me at the moment."

Rone took the spyglass and kneeled, resting it on the rail. He scanned the water behind them and quickly found the set of ships and masts, hazy but large in the captain's massive glass. "They're each of them gunships. Two decks of cannon, it looks like. Perhaps sixty guns each."

"Well, we're still a few hours ahead," Johnny said. He pulled a flask from his pants pocket and unscrewed it, then stared at it a few seconds, eyeing it up and down. He smelled the opening, made a sour face, and then put the flask away. "At least if I got shot in the head today, I wouldn't know the difference."

"The tallest mast is flying green and blue," Rone said, still hunched over. He stood up and looked over at Johnny. "It's Dunneal, then. Or Vindrel, if he broke his promise."

"Promise?" Johnny said.

"He lost a card game with me."

"You had him, and you didn't just shoot him?"

Rone chuckled in response.

"Pierce!" Johnny shouted, still seated. He pulled a compass from his jacket pocket.

"Aye, sir!" Pierce shouted faintly from the wheel.

"Turn us to one-hundred degrees!"

"That's partially into the wind."

"I know that, but we aren't outrunning the bastards going with the wind. Let's see if they can sail as well as us before we turn to give them a fight."

*

The ships were getting larger by mid-afternoon, and they continued to gain even going with a slight cross-wind. The lead ship was indeed one of Catannel's, a three-mast warship that lacked reinforced sides, made for speed rather than pure power. The vessels that had joined it were also flying green jacks, but their second flags were maroon and yellow - ships committed by other fiefdoms in early homage to Catannel.

"They're going to intercept soon, captain," Jasonick said, looking up from his own spyglass. Johnny leaned against a rail, still looking sick and tired.

"It seems they got our number. Steady as she goes, Pierce!" Johnny shouted back over his shoulder.

"Aye, captain!" Pierce shouted back.

"Shouldn't we turn a little more into the wind?" Rone

asked. "If we have our broadside to them, we could get a few shots in before they close, then they'll have a hard time turning about to continue the pursuit."

"You think we'll have to turn and fight?" Charlotte said. She had returned to deck wearing Rone's large hat and now sat on a barrel, drinking tea out of a tin cup.

"Relax," Johnny said. "There should be a continental current a few miles south. If we can catch it before them, we should be alright. Their displacement will hold them back no matter how much sailing power they have."

"You think that'll be enough?" Rone said, watching the little fleet in pursuit.

"We better hope it is," Johnny said seriously.

"Captain! Captain!" The sailor in the crow's nest shouted.

"You need to take a piss or what? I told you to bring up a bucket!" Johnny shouted back.

"Dead ahead, sir! One o'clock!"

"That's not dead ahead, now is it?!" Johnny shouted back at him. He walked over to stand beside the wheel, then leaned over and looked through his spyglass. "Looks like we found a different set of friends," he said, handing the glass over to Rone. Jasonick was already scanning with his own.

Rone saw a few silhouettes in the distance. He wasn't sure if they were floating low, or were still appearing above the horizon, but their masts looked large. One of them was broadside to them, and it had the tale-tell high forecastle and poop of a Draesen galley. "Looks like about seven of them. No oars are down."

"No sails, either," Jasonick said. "They're just floating."

"Why?" Charlotte asked.

"I don't know," Rone leaned down and looked at her. "They could be waiting, or they may have rigged up a foresail or the like. Or they could be resting the slaves."

"The Bergen peninsula isn't too far south of us," Jasonick said. "Maybe they're just waiting for the rest of them."

"Pierce !" Johnny yelled across the ship. "Move us to one-hundred and ten degrees."

"Are you sure!?" he yelled back.

"I'm the bloody captain, of course I'm sure! Pull us to a hundred and ten degrees." Johnny pointed at two sailors, resting against a nearby rail. "Let's trim up and pull the crossbeams accordingly."

"When I suggested we pull further into the wind, I didn't presume it would be into a fleet of warships," Rone said.

"It told you. If there is one thing you can trust me on, it's sailing a ship." Johnny laughed as the boat lurched to starboard, the sails flapping loudly. "Load the cannon and prime your arms!"

"I'll gather the marines up, sir," Jasonick said. "It's going to be a fight!"

Two sailors standing on the main deck grunted in a vicious approval.

"The Gallow wasn't a bad place for labor after all," Rone said.

*

"He put everyone to post too soon," Rone said softly to Charlotte as they watched the dedicated marines assembling on deck. The Draesen ships grew closer, pushed on by countless oars manned by slaves.

Mitha and Delving's marines were a motley bunch. Some were old and grizzled, clearly experienced with piracy. Less experienced men, a few of them young enough to have served as cabin boys on bigger corporate ships, clutched their guns to their chest and sweated even in the cold wind.

"What do you mean?" Charlotte said.

"Johnny's given them far too long to think about the

battle. They'll be pissing themselves with the first volley."

They turned toward the ominous group of galleys in the distance. The Parkitees surged forward, its speed renewed by a shift of wind to their rear. Even so, as the distance closed between the Parkitees and the small fleet of Draesen Empire warships, so did the gap between the Veraland ships and the Parkitees. Tensions were as taught as the sails.

One man and then another would compulsively check his flint or fiddle with the hammer of his pistol, or loosen a cutlass or tighten his belt. A few men held old matchlock arquebuses taken from the ship's official weapons cache, though it was apparent they had not been subject to much inspection or maintenance.

"Old guns," Charlotte said.

"I was thinking the same."

"Will they work? Or are they just for looks?"

"They're for looks. Inquisitors are omnipresent in the Divine Strand. There's a certain reliability to lighting a gun with a match, but it won't matter much. If the hooks are coming out, you're only getting one shot either way before everything goes full melee."

"It seems like everyone ignores the law."

"As much as they can," Rone said. "But you shouldn't underestimate the church."

Pierce stood on the rear deck behind the wheel, looking much the captain with his feather cap and rifle. Meanwhile, Johnny's booming voice could still be heard below on the cannon deck, muffled but with a strange echo from the water. Charlotte pushed herself closer to Rone, feeling his arm wrap around her waist. She gripped her rifle tightly and fell into the tense dance of the marines: shifting her weight from one leg to the other, checking her prime time and again.

The ships grew larger on both sides. It was apparent they

would reach the Draesen craft first. Dark figures, the numerous warriors of that ancient and strange empire, were moving on their decks. Rone had seen them before, even fought them, but he guessed he might be the only one. He prayed silently for courage for the men. The race of the East would terrify any normal-sized man.

"This is going to be bad, isn't it?" Charlotte said quietly.

"Well," Rone said, "Johnny hasn't spoken about any plan, but if he does have one, I wouldn't expect it to include too much fighting, given the circumstances."

"But there will be some, right?"

"Without a doubt. Just stay down as much as you can, and it will be fine."

"Will it?"

"I'll make sure."

They were interrupted by Johnny running up from the cannon deck with a large piece of cloth in his arms. "I almost forgot!" he said. He ran over to the central mast and, with the help of another man, began running the cloth up a rope. When it reached the top, a large green jack unfurled. On the field, a blue square sat, with a yellow circle within.

"Cataling colors?" Rone called out.

"You'll see," Johnny said. "Don't forget to haul up sails after the first cannon shot!" He yelled over his shoulder to Pierce, who stood holding the wheel above.

"Do you just have a box of different flags sitting in your hold?" Charlotte said.

"Yup!" With that, Johnny ducked back into the door and ran down the stairs to the cannon deck.

The sailors up top began to murmur to themselves as the galleys in front of them grew larger at the same time as the gunships behind them spread out into a "V," the smaller, lighter ships moving east and west to cut off any chance of escape. They were perched now between an anvil that was the Draesenith Empire and a rapidly closing hammer.

"We should just haul up and go about," one man, clutching an old matchlock, said. "They may be Isle ships, but they're still from Diederon. Might be a clutch of mercy there."

"I hear ya," his neighbor, holding a similar gun, said. "I hear if they don't want you as a slave, the grey skins will run a spike up your ass and through your mouth, then leave you to die."

"It don't kill you?" the first said.

"Not for days."

"That's enough, you two," Pierce shouted down from above. "Nobody's going to have to fall on anybody's mercy today. Look alive, and we'll come through this just fine."

A splash went up a few hundred yards behind them. The Veraland ships were closing fast and were ready to light up the cannons in their bows in a test of range, and perhaps, a warning. The smaller gunships to the east remained well out of firing range but trimmed their sails as the Parkitees drew nearer to the line of Draesen ships. A few more canons fired, but the ships were still too far away from each other.

The battle, like an invisible beast growling in the stomach of all of them, was hungry for its beginning but remained angrily un-satiated while the Parkitees rolled its straight and windward course toward doom. Rone picked up Johnny's spyglass, left sitting on a barrel nearby, oddly forgotten, and stepped lithely up the stairs to the poop deck. Charlotte followed close behind.

He stared back toward the fleet of the Veraland, taking in the different ships. The lead ship, flying proudly the same flag as the Parkitees (though it's jack was much larger), stood out at the front of the formation, with smaller ships from Masala, Griffing, Sandy Cape, and one from Darfeld that had caught up over the course of the day flanking it.

The lead ship was longer and leaner than what Rone thought of as a typical ship of the line. Its three tall masts urged the ship on to a speed that rivaled that of a clipper, but it was much more heavily armed. He also thought of how heavy their ship was loaded (the Parkitees was, after all, still a shipping vessel), wondering if perhaps they had been willing to throw some cargo overboard, they might have outrun the Veraland fleet.

Rone began to scan the flagship, noting her usual riggings and her steep bow and long body, flanked by gun bays, though only the long guns in the bow were showing. On the front deck, he also saw something that piqued his interest: a large bearded man leaning against the bow rail and looking back with his own spyglass. The ship was still too distant to make out his identity for certain, but he didn't need every detail to know that Vindrel had not kept up his end of the wager.

That'll teach me to hold a gambler to his word, he thought to himself. Rone bowed his head and said a silent prayer. *Dreamer, Lord of the Dragons of Eternity... I named you once, "Lord of Luck," and I shall do so again. Bind my brother to his promise. I have played the game and won, so let me keep my winning this day. Let my dream prevail.*

"It's him, isn't it?" Charlotte said from beside him.

"How did you know?" Rone said.

"You're an easy read," Charlotte said.

Rone sighed. "He's still trying to play cards like before, I suppose. He doesn't know that he doesn't know. It's his flaw. He still thinks he has a card in the deck for me." He stepped away from the aft rail and handed the spyglass to Pierce.

"What do you mean?" Pierce asked as he put the spyglass up to his own eye. After a moment, he said, "Looks like our friend from the docks."

"And the courthouse," Charlotte said.

"He seems to have survived to punish us for our mercy after all," Pierce said. "Well, *your* mercy."

"I wasn't ready to let the man die back then. If it turns out badly, I apologize," Rone said.

"Don't, sir," Pierce said. "I can't fault a man for saving his brother."

"Where did you hear that?" Rone said.

"Men talk," Pierce said.

Rone nodded and walked briskly down the stairs to the main deck, feeling a few prickles of pain in his now healed foot where the stitches had been. Charlotte followed him down and up the other stairs to the bow, where a few marines huddled beneath the foresail. Beyond them, at the other end of an expanse of rippling blue that seemed distant and yet far too close, the Empire ships approached swiftly. Their oars were down, dipping into the water, pushing them forward against the wind.

As they got closer, the details of the shadowy fleet became more concrete. Each ship had deep carvings along their top rails and on their masts. The top few feet of their hulls along the bow were covered in long iron spikes meant to devastate the broad side of a ship during a ram.

The marines began to talk in hushed voices as the details of the enemy became clearer. The Draesenith warriors were huge men with flat grey skin and high pates, long flat faces, and dark eyes that seemed to glitter. They began to howl in a horrid song as they drew nearer, clanging broadswords onto large wooden shields in time with each other, pounding out a steady beat that matched the turning of the oars.

Many of the Draesen held longbows, though they looked somewhat diminished in their great hands. As they closed the distance, flames leaped up from behind the rails like a river of pitch had been lit on fire. The soldiers of the Dreasenith Empire stood still, unaffected and unafraid of the flames.

After a maddeningly tense few minutes of waiting, a shot from the gun deck of the Parkitees set all the actors in the scene into motion. The ship vibrated as the cannon on her bow, the "long nine" Johnny had mentioned, erupted and sent a ball hurtling forward behind a wall of dark smoke. The front of the foremost galley, now pulling just to starboard in preparation for an attack, exploded in a cloud of splinters as the cannonball pierced its iron armor and ripped into its hull. Rone was surprised by the power of the load, flinching as it fired, but also surprised at how high it struck the ship. It was a first shot that was unlikely to sink their enemy, being wholly contained in the top half of the boat.

As they got closer, he could see that the gun deck, stationed above the rows of slaves at the oars, was open to the air. A cannon had fallen through the floor into the midst of the slaves, and their oars stuck out of the water and away from the boat. The galley began to turn as a result, pointing its bow to the Parkitees and also leaving its remaining broadside cannons unused. The ship to its starboard side began to turn as well, angling itself toward the Parkitees in a similar manner, though this one clearly did it with intent. The oars dipped into the water, and the ship moved forward as if it meant to ram them. Another cannon on the Parkitees lit up, and the front of the new galley shuttered under the impact.

Behind Rone, the men jumped into action, and quickly raised the sails. The Parkitees slowed, the iron bow of the enemy closing, but it remained moving forward with its momentum. Rone understood why in a moment, as the marines of both Empire ships moved forward with longbows. Each arrow had a patch of burning pitch attached near its head, and they passed these through the row of flame on their deck. Rone grabbed Charlotte's arm and pulled her down the stairs as the arrows were unleashed, falling and sticking into various places of the ship. Fire caught in a few barrels and leapt onto the shirt of one sailor, but none of the flaming arrows hit the sails.

Suddenly, the door beside Charlotte and Rone burst open, and a familiar face poked out.

"Good gods!" Mineo said, his dazed eyes glaring about at the battle. Rone grabbed his arm and pulled him down into the shadow of the forecastle as a few more flaming arrows zipped past, one lodging itself into the top of the wooden door just above their heads.

"What in the nine worlds are you still doing here!" Rone shouted at him. "I thought you'd be sent off back in the Gallow."

Mineo winced and squinted. "Well, *I* thought I was sleeping off a hangover. Where are we?"

"In the middle of a fight, that's where!" Charlotte said from beneath the staircase.

"Still better than being home with my wife," Mineo said with a shrug.

"Dreamer!" Rone said. "You're a fool if I've ever met one!"

Charlotte darted back up the stair before Rone could stop her and leveled her rifle at the ship on the port side. She shot along with the other marines on deck, who had somehow managed to avoid all of the arrow fire. A few men on board the Eastern ship went down with a shriek, and Charlotte darted back down the stair to reload, horn in hand.

The Parkitees began floating past the ship on its port side, and the spikes lacing the front of the galley scratched across the rails, sending splinters flying in every direction. A few brave Draesen warriors jumped off the bow of their ship onto the deck of the Parkitees, or swung over on a rigging rope, pikes in hand. They landed among the men of the Parkitees like giants, all of them standing a head taller than the sailors. Only Johnny himself, who was as good as half-giant, would have been able to look any of them in the eye. Rone leaned his musket down and drew his sword and pistol. The canons of the Parkitees fired from the broadside, and more wooden shards exploded from the hull of the attacker.

Rone ran at the first colossal pikeman in front of him, parrying the long downward thrust of the mail-armored Draesen with his backsword, forcing the point into the hard oak of the deck. He then stood on the pike with his left foot. The enemy unhanded his weapon and let it drop to the deck with a loud clack.

The Draesen stepped back with surprise and drew his own curved sword from a scabbard at his hip, scowling at Rone as he did so. The marine slashed wildly, never able to fully connect as Rone moved around him in circles. Rone, at last, stepped nimbly past his opponent during a hard overhand slash and struck him in the back of his neck with the tip of his backsword. The warrior collapsed in a spray of blood, grasping at the wound below his ear. He began to scream in his strange language, but Rone had already moved on.

He stepped forward to the next grey-skinned man, who already had a long scimitar drawn and held it forward in a right-foot leaning stance. Rone suddenly longed for a more substantial weapon than his trusted backsword as the warrior attacked. He had experience in battle and displayed it with a series of well-aimed and controlled thrusts while he kept strictly to a balanced fighting style.

Rone shuffled around him in circles, keeping his weight forward on his right foot, ready for the killing thrust if he saw an opening. Rone parried and dodged with calm precision, but was reminded of his limitations every time he tried to step past the giant's outer arc and was treated to a shield bash or whirling cut. Rone understood that the swordsman was, with the strokes of his blade, pushing him into a corner of the railing. The guns in the deck below them roared to life again, pushing the Parkitees away and crushing the hull at the front of the galley. Its iron-spiked bow began to droop as the ship drifted away, chunks of wood and stray boards falling into the sea.

Another flurry of arrows rained down, this time from the crippled ship off the Parkitees's starboard. Rone quickly turned his body to miss one, and his opposition closed in with a slash that cut his shirt and narrowly missed the flesh of his ribcage. Rone jumped back and saw Charlotte being attacked by a pikeman. She kept him at a distance by parrying his mocking blows with her rifle as he tried to push past and put the single-edged spear to use. Rone threw himself to his left and shot his pistol, not nearly so much aiming as hoping, at Charlotte's attacker, who collapsed in a grunt as the ball hit his leg. A nearby marine saw the Draesen bend down and took advantage of the wound. He moved past the blade of the spear and smashed the Draesen's clavicle with a cutlass, spraying the deck with fresh blood.

Rone's adversary had not let up, however, and he swung down on Rone with a powerful overhand stroke. In a fit of confusion, shock, and fear, Rone threw up his left hand, and the scimitar hit the stock of his pistol a few inches from his knuckles. Rone fell to his knees with the force of the blow, crying out as his wrist twisted with the impact. His opponent pulled back for the killing blow but found his blade stuck in the tight-grained wood of the pistol. Before he could adjust position and free himself, Rone was pulling the off-balance warrior down onto the tip of his sword. It split the rings of the Draesen's mail coif and entered his neck. Rone rolled with his opponent's immense weight, pushing him down on the deck. With a gasp, the Draesen closed his eyes and went limp.

Rone looked around to see a few dying fires from the arrows, which seemed unable to coax the old and well-treated oak slats of the deck to flame. Seawater was being dumped on the few bits of fire that managed to survive. The Parkitees was pulling away from the two ships, though the impact had significantly slowed her inertia. The cannons on the starboard side lit up again, pelting the already crippled Draesen ship with fresh lead, all of the impacts high above the watertight hull, as the few enemy marines on the Parkitees's deck scrambled to get back on board their own ship.

Charlotte shuddered as one sailor, a thin and short man, probably a boy among the race of giants, made a running leap to return home and fell short, his hands flailing wildly for purchase among the shredded remains of the galley hull before he fell into the sea. The sailors of the Parkitees scrambled to the ropes and began loosening the sails. As they filled with the wind the ship sprang back to life, surging off past the two galleys.

Rone, astonished, realized that despite their damage, they had almost totally avoided cannon fire. He snapped back to the moment at the cries of an unfamiliar marine nearby, clutching at a wound on his leg. Blood was surging up between his fingers. Rone quickly tore the man's sleeve off and wrapped it tightly around the leg wound, making a quick tourniquet. He stood up and could finally see just what Johnny's plan had been. The small fleet of the Draesenith Empire now blocked Vindrel, along with the rest of the Veraland ships, from continuing their pursuit. Already ships flying green were breaking their formation to engage the galleys, and the flagship was forcing a hard turn to avoid the two galleys the Parkitees had sped past. Those Draesen ships, though crippled, were now moving to engage the new threat, the warriors packing the decks screaming a new song.

The two smaller ships that had moved east to block the Parkitees's retreat were well wide of the Empire ships, but Rone watched as they turned hard about to assist their comrades, the green and red jack of Masala flying high up above their mainsails.

Johnny emerged from the gun deck, covered in soot, but smiling. "Well, that's as close as they come. Was there any fighting up top?"

"A little," Rone answered, "but it was nothing we couldn't handle. One significant injury. We're going to have to fix some railing, though." He looked over to see Mineo push himself up, debris and shards of wood falling away. He had apparently remained where Rone had placed him throughout the entire fight.

"Aww," Johnny said, looking at the starboard deck rails, which lay in pieces on the deck proper. "Where am I going to lean over and vomit when I get seasick?"

The cannon fire continued behind them, but within minutes relaxation and a sense of relief seemed to permeate the crew. The battle was behind them, and the wind was in their sails. The sounds of cannons began to fade into to the sounds of the sea itself. Johnny went into his quarters and returned with a full bottle of whiskey.

"To long life between the hammer and the anvil!" he shouted, then took a long drink. The crew that was still assembled above decks cheered in response. Mineo walked over and held out his hand as if expecting the captain to share. Johnny jerked the bottle toward himself and took another swig. "Get your own!" The men laughed.

"It's grog for you," Pierce said from up top, "Never try to drink the captain's whiskey."

"I'll deal with you soon enough!" Johnny said, "I'm missing a bottle of Drachman Sour, thanks to you!" He raised his middle finger to the first mate.

Charlotte pushed herself under Rone's arm and leaned against him. He sighed deeply, letting go of the tension of the moment and leaning on her. He looked down to see her smiling back as if the bloody struggle minutes before had never happened.

"Now, pitch these stowaways overboard!" Johnny yelled, kicking a nearby corpse. Laughter answered him. Rone walked over and picked up the Dreasen's long scimitar, thinking of how much trouble the man had given him. His dead opponent stared back at him with blank, yellow eyes.

Charlotte gently rubbed his back. He felt the steel, which was keen and smooth, with a forging pattern like the grain of a piece of wood. Suddenly, he felt something else from the steel, something imperceptible, and he threw it down.

"It doesn't feel right," he said. "I don't want it."

He pulled his pistol from his belt and looked at it. The small stock was broken apart, and the handle would no longer contain the lock and barrel. He pulled the broken stock off and tossed it to the side, then stuffed the rest of the gun in his belt.

A few of the marines busied themselves with the robbing of the bodies. Armor, clothes, bags, and weapons were laid in a heap as each bloody body was stripped down, then picked up by its hands and feet and thrown unceremoniously overboard.

"Shouldn't we say something?" Charlotte whispered into Rone's ear.

"Like what?" he whispered back.

"Last rites? A prayer? Don't these men deserve a proper blessing and burial?"

"A Draesen burial is something we can't give them, nor would I ever pray to their gods – they're cursed. Silence and a burial at sea are the best we can offer, I think."

"Perhaps I can say a prayer to Verbus?"

"It couldn't hurt," Rone said. "But if they were living, they would be enraged. They believe the soul returns to the body. That is no mercy!"

"You're a strange man, Rone."

"You're the only one questioning their burial. It's *you* that's strange."

"Don't try to turn this around on me, you scoundrel," she said, a smile cracking her ash-greyed face. "You are a very, very strange man, but I still love you. And I know you love me." She stood on her toes and kissed his jaw. His face, taught from the tension of a fight, relaxed at the touch.

"It makes it complicated."

"You'll have to deal with it."

Rone wiped some grit from her face with his thumb and sighed.

"What is it?"

"I think your importance in all this might have dropped somewhat. War is here."

"Lucky for me, my partner is a fierce warrior."

"Partner?"

"Well, I can't very well keep calling you my bodyguard, or my servant, can I?"

"Suit yourself," Rone said, raising his eyebrows in a kind of faux disregard.

"I'm starting to do just that," Charlotte said and hugged him around his waist.

End of Book II

About the Author

David Van Dyke Stewart is an author, musician, YouTuber, and educator who currently lives in rural California with his wife and children.

He is the author of *Muramasa: Blood Drinker, Water of Awakening*, the *Needle Ash* series, and *The Crown of Sight,* as well as numerous novellas, essays, and short stories. He is also the primary performer in the music project *David V. Stewart's Zul.*

You can find his YouTube channel at http://www.youtube.com/rpmfidel where he creates content on music education, literary analysis, movie analysis, philosophy, and logic.

Sign up to his mailing list at http://dvspress.com/list for a free book and advance access to future projects. You can email any questions or concerns to stu@dvspress.com.

Be sure to check http://davidvstewart.com and http://dvspress.com for news and free samples of all his books.

Printed in Great Britain
by Amazon